"What are *you* doing here?"

Lily had practically skipped down the hall to Sonia's office and now had bumped into a wall she hadn't encountered on her first tour of the house. One that was solid. *Warm.*

"That's funny." One dark eyebrow lifted. "I was about to ask you the same question."

If it was funny, then why wasn't he smiling?

"I'm going to do some prep work."

Her explanation was met with silence. Lily tried again. "Scrub the walls. Tape around the windows and trim—"

"I know what prep work is," Brendan interrupted. "But why are you in *here?*"

Lily took a deep breath. Prayed for patience. "Because this is the room I'll be painting first."

"No."

Manager or not, she was getting a little tired of the man's high-handed ways.

"My employer—" Lily couldn't help but press down on the word "—gave me a list of the rooms she wanted me to paint, and this office happens to be one of them. Is there a problem?"

Yes. There was.

Books by Kathryn Springer

Love Inspired

Tested by Fire
Her Christmas Wish
By Her Side
For Her Son's Love
A Treasure Worth Keeping
Hidden Treasures
Family Treasures
Jingle Bell Babies
*A Place to Call Home
*Love Finds a Home
*The Prodigal Comes Home
The Prodigal's Christmas Reunion
*Longing for Home
*The Promise of Home
The Soldier's Newfound Family
*Making His Way Home
†The Bachelor Next Door

*Mirror Lake
†Castle Falls

Love Inspired Single Title

Front Porch Princess
Hearts Evergreen
 *"A Match Made
 for Christmas"*
Picket Fence Promises
The Prince Charming List

KATHRYN SPRINGER

is a lifelong Wisconsin resident. Growing up in a "newspaper" family, she spent long hours as a child plunking out stories on her mother's typewriter and hasn't stopped writing since. She loves to write inspirational romance because it allows her to combine her faith in God with her love of a happy ending.

The Bachelor Next Door

Kathryn Springer

Recycling programs
for this product may
not exist in your area.

 ™ LOVE INSPIRED BOOKS

ISBN-13: 978-0-373-81775-7

THE BACHELOR NEXT DOOR

Copyright © 2014 by Kathryn Springer

www.Harlequin.com

Printed in U.S.A.

He is like a tree planted by streams of water,
Which yields its fruit in season
And whose leaf does not wither.
Whatever he does prospers.
—*Psalms* 1:3

Chapter One

He didn't have time for this.

Brendan Kane followed the path of destruction down the hall to the living room, where tiny pieces of white foam scattered across the hardwood floor made it look as if an early snowfall had swept across Michigan's Upper Peninsula. The trail wound between the coffee table and leather recliner and disappeared behind the sofa.

Brendan knelt down for a better look. Sure enough, peering at him over a barricade of stolen goods was the perpetrator of the latest crime spree. A slightly overweight basset hound happily stripping the remaining leaves from the branch of a silk ficus his mother had rescued from the curb just moments before it was devoured by the steel jaws of the garbage truck.

Because rescuing things was part of Sunni's M.O., which was how Brendan had ended up with Missy, a troublesome canine who preferred leather shoes, artificial plants and, yes, even the occasional sofa pillow, over rawhide chews.

"There are laws against vandalism, you know." He scowled at the dog but she ignored him. It reminded Brendan of Sunni's response when he'd told her that he was too busy to care for a pet.

A few months ago, his mother had started volunteering at the local animal shelter, and it had become her personal mission to find homes for all the stray dogs and cats that came in on her watch. Sunni was gaining quite a reputation in Castle Falls for her ability to match an animal with just the right owner. But so far, when it came to her oldest son, she was 0 for 3.

Brendan had been waiting for her to realize that *he* was the common denominator in all the failed relationships.

"This is strike three, you know." And he was out. "You're going to have to chew someone else out of house and—" Brendan paused as his cell phone began to blast the theme song from *Mission: Impossible,* signaling an incoming call from his youngest brother.

Brendan stabbed at the green circle on the screen. "What?"

"I'm fine. Thanks for asking." Aiden's low chuckle rattled in his ear. "Are you busy?"

"I'm always busy." Brendan narrowed his eyes at the basset hound. She'd dropped the ficus branch and was eyeing his shoelaces as if they were the artificial plants and, yes, even the occasional sofa pillow, over rawhide chews.

"There are laws against vandalism, you know." He scowled at the dog but she ignored him. It reminded Brendan of Sunni's response when he'd told her that he was too busy to care for a pet.

A few months ago, his mother had started volunteering at the local animal shelter, and it had become her personal mission to find homes for all the stray dogs and cats that came in on her watch. Sunni was gaining quite a reputation in Castle Falls for her ability to match an animal with just the right owner. But so far, when it came to her oldest son, she was 0 for 3.

Brendan had been waiting for her to realize that *he* was the common denominator in all the failed relationships.

"This is strike three, you know." And he was out. "You're going to have to chew someone else out of house and—" Brendan paused as his cell phone began to blast the theme song from *Mission: Impossible,* signaling an incoming call from his youngest brother.

Brendan stabbed at the green circle on the screen. "What?"

"I'm fine. Thanks for asking." Aiden's low chuckle rattled in his ear. "Are you busy?"

"I'm always busy." Brendan narrowed his eyes at the basset hound. She'd dropped the ficus branch and was eyeing his shoelaces as if they were the

Chapter One

He didn't have time for this.

Brendan Kane followed the path of destruction down the hall to the living room, where tiny pieces of white foam scattered across the hardwood floor made it look as if an early snowfall had swept across Michigan's Upper Peninsula. The trail wound between the coffee table and leather recliner and disappeared behind the sofa.

Brendan knelt down for a better look. Sure enough, peering at him over a barricade of stolen goods was the perpetrator of the latest crime spree. A slightly overweight basset hound happily stripping the remaining leaves from the branch of a silk ficus his mother had rescued from the curb just moments before it was devoured by the steel jaws of the garbage truck.

Because rescuing things was part of Sunni's M.O., which was how Brendan had ended up with Missy, a troublesome canine who preferred leather shoes, next item on the buffet. "Don't even think about it," he muttered.

"Don't think about what?"

"I wasn't talking to you."

"Okay," Aiden said mildly. "Then who *are* you talking to?"

Busted.

"No one."

"Disturbing. And proof you need to get out more."

"Fine. I was talking to…Missy." Brendan was forced to be honest, although he hated giving his kid brother any ammunition that could potentially be used against him in the future.

"Are you kidding?" Aiden hooted. Obviously forgetting the fact that he was four years younger, two inches shorter and had yet to beat Brendan in hand-to-hand sibling combat. "Liam and I didn't think she'd last a week."

Brendan silently counted backward. "You were right."

The statement was followed by a whistle that threatened to pierce his left eardrum. "Have you broken the news to Mom?"

"Not yet."

"Can I watch?"

"Very funny." Brendan swept up a handful of damp leaf debris. "I tried to tell her this was destined to fail."

Missy cast a reproachful look in his direction, took a few waddling steps forward and leaped onto the couch. No easy feat for an animal roughly the size and shape of the pillow she'd recently shredded.

"You know Mom," Aiden said. "She wants everyone to be happy."

"Then why isn't she leaving dogs on *your* doorstep?"

Brendan relocated an African violet from the windowsill to the stone ledge above the fireplace. Just in case.

"Maybe she thinks you need the practice," his brother said cheerfully.

Brendan scowled. "What kind of practice?"

"Uh…the commitment kind?"

"I am committed." To the business he'd poured his heart and soul into for the past fifteen years. At sixteen, Brendan had saved Castle Falls Outfitters from bankruptcy. Ten years later, he'd doubled its annual profit. And any day now, if everything went according to plan, he would be signing a contract with a large sporting-goods chain, making their custommade canoes available throughout the Midwest.

No one seemed to realize that kind of responsibility didn't leave a whole lot of time for anything else. Not that Brendan was complaining. It would take a lifetime to repay the debt he owed Sunni Mason, a woman who'd taken in three aspiring juvenile delinquents when they'd had nowhere else to go.

"Or…Mom knows you practically live in your office, and she doesn't want you to be lonely."

"Lonely." When Brendan barely had a minute to

himself? He worked out of an office at their mother's house, and even though his two younger brothers had converted storage space above the garage into a spacious apartment, they spent more time hanging out at his place than they did their own.

"You've heard the word, right?" Aiden laughed. "It's one of those pesky little things people sometimes refer to as emotions."

Brendan rolled his eyes. He didn't have time for those, either.

A car door slammed, and he glanced at the clock. Five o'clock on the dot. Sonia, affectionately known as Sunni to the people who loved her, was always punctual.

"I have to go."

"Wait—"

Brendan hung up the phone. A split second later, he heard Sunni humming the chorus of a familiar praise song as she made her way up the sidewalk.

Missy tipped her nose toward the ceiling and let out a mournful howl.

The humming stopped.

Great.

"Tattletale," he grumbled.

The dog ignored him—naturally—and launched herself off the sofa. All four paws shot out in different directions on the hardwood floor like the points on a compass, and yet she *still* managed to beat him to the front door.

"Hi, sweetheart."

Looking, Brendan noted wryly, not at him but at the overweight basset hound nibbling on the laces of her pink hiking boots.

"How are you two getting along?"

Also directed at the dog.

Brendan decided to answer the question anyway. Since he was the one who had opposable thumbs—and actually *could* speak. "She shredded my favorite tie yesterday."

"Good girl, Missy," his mother whispered. "I never did care for that tie."

"You're the one who bought it for me," Brendan pointed out.

"Only because I knew *you'd* like it." Bending down to give Missy's glossy head a pat, Sunni spotted the dog bed and basket of toys stacked neatly beside the door. Shook her head. "What seems to be the problem?"

She didn't add the words *this time*. They were implied.

"Missy is a great dog." A slight exaggeration, considering her penchant for turning everything into a chew toy. "But I just can't give her the attention she deserves." Brendan braced himself for the fall-out. Again.

Sunni smiled. *Smiled.* "I understand."

"Really?" Because he remembered saying the same thing the day she'd dropped off Raquel, the incontinent Yorkie, and Bette Davis, a Doberman pinscher who'd hidden under the bed whenever someone knocked on the door, totally undermining his mother's claim that she'd be a great watchdog.

"I'll take Missy with me to church tonight and introduce her to Ed Wilson. His wife passed away a few months ago, and I heard him tell Pastor Tamblin the house is too quiet."

Brendan's eyes narrowed.

That was it?

"She'll be happier," he said. "You know that, right?"

"But will you?" Sunni murmured.

Brendan took a moment to think about that.

Yes. Yes, he would.

"I'll put this stuff in the car for you. I'm sure Missy and Mr. Wilson will get along really well." He grabbed the box of toys before she could change her mind.

"Thank you, sweetheart. I have some last-minute packing to finish up before choir practice starts." Sunni followed him outside to the gray Subaru parked in front of the house, Missy happily chugging along at her heels.

Brendan popped open the trunk and blinked. "What's all this?"

"Paint." His mom grinned. "The house is long overdue for a makeover. I figured the best time to tackle a project that size is while I'm away on my birthday cruise."

Brendan couldn't argue with the timing *or* her claim that the rooms would benefit from a fresh coat of paint. The walls were still the same color they'd been when he'd moved from Detroit to Castle Falls at the age of fifteen. Six months after he and his brothers unpacked their belongings, Sunni had been more worried about keeping the bank from foreclosing on the house than she had about decorating it.

"Mark which color goes in which room." Brendan silently rearranged his schedule to accommodate a new project. "I can't promise I'll have it finished by the time you get home, but I'll do my best."

"Oh, you don't have to do a thing, sweetheart. I made other arrangements."

Brendan slowly pivoted to face her. "What kind of other arrangements?"

"You're always saying how busy you are—" Sunni flashed a smile that rivaled the July sunshine for brightness "—so I hired someone."

Lily Michaels tapped on the brake, and her car rolled to a stop on a crack in the asphalt where the road ended and a narrow wooden bridge began. Leaning forward, she squinted at a hand-painted sign framed between two pine trees on the other side of the river.

Castle Falls Outfitters.

She pulled in a breath and held it.

This was it. The beginning of a brand-new adventure.

Or the biggest mistake of your life.

Lily refused to listen to that negative inner

voice—a gruff baritone that sounded suspiciously like her father's.

But the contract in her purse, signed by Sonia Mason, proved that God was directing her steps. Even if Lily had never actually *met* the woman in person.

She glanced at the clock on the dashboard and sighed.

It didn't look as if she'd have the opportunity to meet her very first client today, either. Lily's plan to get an early start that morning had been sabotaged by a nail that had found its way into her tire as she'd backed out of the driveway of her apartment complex.

Please make yourself at home if I'm not there when you arrive, Sunni had written in her last email.

At home.

Another answer to prayer.

There were no hotels in Castle Falls, so Sunni had offered the use of her guest room until she returned from her Caribbean cruise. Lily had agreed to the arrangement without hesitation. The town was too far from Traverse City to commute back and forth—and too far away for her father to drop by.

Something he'd been doing on a daily basis for the past few weeks. Nolan Michaels made no secret of the fact he wasn't happy with Lily's "impulsive decision" to change careers, even temporarily.

Her hands tightened around the steering wheel as the wooden bridge shuddered beneath the weight of her compact car. Once she was safely on the other side, it was easier to appreciate the unspoiled beauty of her surroundings. On the map, the river had been a tiny blue thread embroidered along an edge of national forest in Michigan's Upper Peninsula. She caught a flash of sapphire through the trees and heard the water humming a cheerful melody as it spilled over the rocks.

Lily couldn't wait to explore. If there was one thing she'd learned from Shelby, it was to view every day as a gift from God, meant to be unwrapped and enjoyed.

The thick hedge of trees began to thin out, and the late-afternoon sun winked off a metal roof. Rounding a curve, Lily drove past a large aluminum pole building and caught a glimpse of a rustic cabin tucked in a stand of trees behind it.

Sonia had mentioned she ran a home-based business, but Lily had been too busy concentrating on her own list of last-minute details to ask questions.

When the house came into view, she realized she probably should have.

The Craftsman-style Foursquare, dating back to the '50s, wore a shaggy coat of iron-gray paint. Its patchwork roof dipped low over the front porch like an old tweed cap, shading the windows from the sun. It looked to Lily as if the pink petunias planted along the sidewalk were nodding a welcome as she hopped out of the car.

Underneath the sisal welcome mat, she found a

key to the front door. The small piece of metal felt heavy in the palm of Lily's hand.

Although she had requested photographs of the rooms she'd be renovating, Sunni had neglected to send any. Now, after seeing the *outside* of the house, Lily wondered if the oversight had been deliberate.

Well, there's only one way to find out, isn't there?

She fit the key in the lock and pushed the door open. One step forward and Lily found herself standing in a tunnel of blue-and-white gingham check, the pattern broken only by a line of bright red, wallpaper roosters marching along the strip of baseboard.

Following the roosters into the kitchen, Lily clapped one hand over her mouth to muffle a burst of laughter.

Yellow plaid wallpaper and…sheep. Dozens of them, stenciled from floor to ceiling on all four walls and grazing between the cupboards.

By the time Lily walked into the living room and saw the tangerine walls, she decided this was going to be fun. The interior might be a bit outdated, but overall, the house had a personality as warm and inviting as a flannel shirt in January.

She opened the last door at the end of the hall and felt a jolt of surprise.

Sparse and utilitarian, the only furnishings were a navy blue wingback chair and a desk that, oddly enough, didn't face the row of windows overlooking the river. Unlike the rest of the rooms, there were no houseplants or knickknacks on the shelves. No pictures on the walls. Even though Lily had never met Sonia, she couldn't imagine the woman spending her days in an office that lacked the warmth of the rest of her home.

Lily smiled.

She'd start the transformation here.

Brendan was late.

True, he probably shouldn't have scheduled an appointment on the day his mother had to be at the airport, but there should have been plenty of time for both...if Brendan hadn't been forced to take a detour because of road construction. And if the detour hadn't been a back road with more twists and turns than a corn maze. Which meant Domita Peterson had probably gotten tired of waiting for him and left.

He hadn't been able to reach her by phone, not an uncommon occurrence given the unreliable cellphone reception in the area. Ordinarily, Liam and Aiden would have been available to greet a potential customer, but they'd left that morning for a weekend-long camping trip to test one of Liam's new designs.

Brendan could only hope Mrs. Peterson had more patience than *he* did.

The frustration he'd been battling distilled into relief at the sight of an unfamiliar vehicle parked in the driveway. As he pulled up next to it and got out of the car, a woman rounded the corner of the house.

A *young* woman.

When Domita Peterson had called to request a meeting, she'd mentioned that she wanted to give her husband a canoe as a gift for his retirement. Brendan hadn't anticipated she would be in her mid-twenties, closer to *his* age than his mother's. With a face and figure guaranteed to draw a second glance.

Although the combination of faded jeans, a bright pink T-shirt and golden-blond hair separated into two ponytails made her look more girl-next-door than trophy wife.

"I'm sorry I'm late." Brendan kept his expression neutral.

Reminded himself that the woman's personal business wasn't any of *his*. "Why don't we go inside, where it's cooler?"

The woman's eyes, an unusual shade of blue-violet that reminded Brendan of the wildflowers that carpeted the woods every spring, widened in response to the suggestion.

Maybe she'd been expecting that the Castle Falls Outfitters' office would be housed in something other than a…house. It wouldn't be the first time a potential customer had a difficult time reconciling the craftsmanship of their work with the *place* where they worked.

Brendan made it halfway down the sidewalk when he realized this potential customer wasn't following him. He glanced over his shoulder.

"Is something wrong?"

"I...I think you have me confused with some-one else."

Brendan frowned. "Aren't you Domita Peterson? My six o'clock appointment?"

The woman shook her head, and the movement sent the twin ponytails dancing.

"I'm Lily Michaels—the painter. And you are..."

Someone who plans to have a little chat with his mother as soon as possible, Brendan thought grimly.

Except that he couldn't. Because at that very moment, Sunni was on a cruise ship bound for the Caribbean.

Chapter Two

Lily waited for the man to fill in the blank.

He didn't *look* dangerous, but a girl couldn't be too careful nowadays. Dark hair. Eyes the velvet-blue of an evening sky. The chiseled features would have been improved by a smile, but he was attractive in a brooding, Mr. Darcy kind of way.

"Brendan Kane," he finally said.

Now it looked as if *he* was waiting for something. Lily stitched the pieces of their brief conversation together in her mind, trying to make sense of them. He'd apologized for being late. And the flash of disbelief in his eyes when she'd introduced herself meant that he'd been expecting someone else—a Domita Somebody or Another.

"Did you have an appointment with one of Sonia Mason's employees?" she ventured. "Because I think everyone left for the day."

"Not all of them." A wry smile kicked up the corner of his lips, and Lily felt a corresponding kick in the general vicinity of her heart. Flustered, she lowered her gaze—and spotted the logo embroidered on the pocket of his polo shirt.

Castle Falls Outfitters.

Brendan Kane *was* one of the employees.

"I…" *Feel like an idiot?* "I'm sorry. I didn't realize you worked for Sonia Mason, too. She hired me a few weeks ago to do some painting while she's on vacation, but I'm afraid I don't know much about her business." Lily forced a smile. "I should have asked more questions."

"You aren't the only one," he muttered.

She wasn't sure how to decipher the cryptic statement, but something in Brendan Kane's tone told her that he wasn't pleased by the situation. Was he afraid she was going to get in his way?

Or was he the type of person who thought her type of work was unnecessary? Frivolous?

Anyone can splash paint on a wall, Lily. You're wasting your talents…and your time. If you take a leave of absence now, someone else is going to take your place. Everything you've worked to accomplish will be gone.

Her father's parting words had left their mark. In Nolan Michaels's world, the number of hours a person worked, combined with the number of digits that made up their annual salary, equaled success. The fact that Lily was being considered for a promotion had made it even more difficult for him to understand.

It didn't even seem to matter that Lily's change in careers, in order to help out a friend in need, was temporary.

If only her father had seen the expression on Shelby's face when Lily had offered to take over her custom painting until she regained her strength after being diagnosed with Lyme disease.

Hope.

Lily folded the memory into a smile and tucked it away for safekeeping.

She'd made the right decision.

"If you'll excuse me. I have a few things to unload before it gets dark." Lily skirted the six-foot-two, blue-eyed obstacle on the sidewalk. She could only hope her and Brendan Kane's paths wouldn't cross very often in the next ten days....

"I'll give you a hand."

Lily dragged in a breath, ready to decline, but the masculine—and all-too-appealing—scent of fresh air and freshly laundered cotton filled her lungs. And did strange things to her vocal cords. All she could manage was a...squeak.

A squeak Brendan must have taken as consent, because he reached into the trunk of the car and pulled out a box filled with drop cloths.

"You can set the bins in the hallway." Lily found her voice as she wrestled a folding ladder from the backseat. "I'll organize everything later."

"What's this?"

Peeking over the top of the door, she saw him

holding her pink paisley Vera Bradley weekender, a birthday gift from Shelby, at arm's length. The way a person might hold a plastic bag bound for the curb. Or a package that had suddenly started to tick.

Lily hesitated, wondering if this was a trick question. "My suitcase?"

"Suitcase." He frowned, clearly suspicious.

They do come in more than colors than black and navy blue, Lily thought. Then promptly asked God's forgiveness for the uncharitable thought.

"Don't worry about that one." Setting the ladder down, she held out her hand, ready to rescue the bag from his grip. "I'll take it upstairs."

"Upstairs?" The frown deepened.

And he was *still* attractive.

Life, Lily thought, just wasn't fair.

"You're not staying here." It came out sounding more like a statement than a question.

"Sonia offered the use of her guest room while she's on vacation," Lily explained. "Paint the Town is based in Traverse City, so it would have been too far to drive back and forth."

"I'm surprised you accepted a job way up here in the middle of nowhere." A muscle working in that chiseled jaw tightened at the words.

Lily didn't know why it mattered where she stayed. But if Brendan Kane was Sonia's manager, as she suspected, he probably resented the fact that his employer hadn't kept him in the loop.

"I didn't have the luxury of turning down the job."

She pressed out a smile. "And Sonia assured me that I have all the qualifications she's been looking for."

The blue eyes closed briefly, and Lily could only guess what the man was thinking of. Tossing her offensive floral luggage in the river? Ordering her off the property?

She decided not to wait around to find out.

"I appreciate your help, but I can handle the rest of it." Plucking the suitcase from his hand, Lily headed to the front door. This time—*thank You, God*—he didn't follow.

She practically sprinted up the stairs to the second floor and took refuge in the spare room at the end of the hall. Number four on the makeover list. Sonia had requested something lighter than the existing hunter-green walls and burgundy trim, which gave the room a distinctly masculine feel.

Lily unpacked her suitcase and matched each item of clothing to a plastic hanger in the closet. She read through Sonia's list and matched paint chips to the appropriate rooms.

In other words, she was stalling.

After an hour or so, when she figured the coast was clear, Lily padded downstairs.

Anticipation began to wash away the memory of her encounter with Brendan the Brusque. She sorted through the cans of paint until she came to the words *chai tea* scribbled on the lid. Rich vanilla, with a subtle vein of gold, would provide the perfect frame for the window overlooking the river.

Lily practically skipped down the hall to Sonia's office. And bumped into a wall she hadn't encountered on her first tour of the house. Solid. *Warm.*

She stumbled backward. "What are *you* doing here?"

"That's funny." One dark eyebrow lifted. "I was about to ask you the same question."

If it was funny, then why wasn't he smiling?

"I'm going to do some prep work."

Her explanation was met with silence. Lily tried again. "Scrub the walls. Tape around the windows and trim—"

"I know what prep work is," Brendan interrupted. "But why are you in *here?*"

Lily took a deep breath. Prayed for patience. "Because this is the room I'll be painting first."

"No."

Manager or not, she was getting a little tired of the man's high-handed ways.

"My employer—" Lily couldn't help but press down on the word "—gave me a list of the rooms she wanted me to paint and this office happens to be one of them. Is there a problem?"

Yes. There was.

In fact, Brendan had started a list of his own.

Beginning with the fact that Sunni had neglected to mention the person she'd hired for *Castle Falls Outfitters: Makeover Edition* was a leggy blonde with violet eyes.

Or that she'd be living upstairs.

Maybe his mother hadn't had an ulterior motive. Maybe a woman—a *beautiful* woman—in her mid-twenties who lived in a city over half a day's drive from Castle Falls had been the only painter available.

Yeah. Right.

"This isn't Sunni's office." Brendan speared a hand through his hair. "It's mine."

"Who is Sunni?"

"Sunni Mason…my mother." The words had gotten easier to say over the years. Unlike his brothers, Brendan still remembered the woman who'd given birth to them. Even if those memories weren't the kind a person was eager to share.

"But—" Lily's forehead puckered "—I thought you were the manager."

"I am. I'm also the son. My two younger brothers work here, too, but they're gone for a few days." Brendan could only imagine what his siblings' reactions would be when they returned and discovered what Sunni had done. "We all take care of a different aspect of the business. Liam designs the boats, Aiden tests them and I find people to buy them. From *this* office," he couldn't help but add.

Some unidentifiable emotion flared in Lily's eyes. "Do you *live* here—in this house—too?"

Brendan shook his head. "In a cabin behind the shop. I like my privacy." It had to be said. "So you understand why this won't work. It's a small space, and there isn't room for both of us."

"Oh, I understand." The corners of her watercolor-pink lips twitched.

Was she trying not to smile? Okay, maybe that had sounded like something the sheriff in a cheesy old black-and-white Western might say—*this town isn't big enough for the two of us*—but it also happened to be the truth.

Lily took two steps forward and paused in the doorway. Tipped her head. "Do you like it?"

"Do I like what?"

"Your office."

Did he like… What kind of question was that? Brendan shrugged. "It's an office."

"The place where you spend the majority of your day?"

"Yes." He wondered where she was going with this. "When I'm working, I'm focused on work." Even if the walls were—Brendan took a quick inventory of the room—dark green with a brownish fleck.

Kind of like the algae that coated the rocks along the riverbank.

"I really don't care about the color of the walls." He closed the conversation with a polite smile.

Lily didn't move. "What are your regular business hours?"

"There's no such thing when you own your own business."

Something Brendan had discovered the first time he'd driven through the night to personally deliver an order, and as the owner of a small business, she should have known that, as well. "Why?"

"If you don't want me in here when you're working," Lily said sweetly. "I need to know when you *won't* be."

"I thought we already established that I don't want you to paint my office."

"I'm sorry, but it really isn't a question of what you want, is it? You might be the manager, but Sonia is my boss." Lily held up a square of flowered stationery that looked as if it had been cut from the same material as her suitcase. "And this office happens to be on the list of rooms she asked me to paint. If you have a problem with that, I suggest you take it up with her."

Brendan would have—if Sunni had taken her cell phone. Or her laptop. But *someone* had insisted she leave all means of communication behind in order to truly "get away from it all."

He mentally kicked himself.

"I start work at seven in the morning and stay as long as necessary." He pushed the words out slowly, one by one, hoping she could take a hint.

"When is your day off? I'll try and work around that."

"It...varies." Brendan tried to remember the last time he'd taken a day off. "A lot."

"Are you always this difficult?"

"Are you?" he shot back.

Lily had the audacity to grin.

"I guess you'll find out, won't you?"

* * *

Things weren't turning out quite the way Lily had planned.

She rolled onto her back in the twin bed and stared up at the ceiling, mentally sifting through the emails she and Sonia Mason had exchanged over the past few weeks.

The boys are in and out, Lily vaguely remembered the woman saying. What her client had failed to mention, however, was the fact they were *her* boys. Lily had assumed it was simply an affectionate term for her employees.

Whatever her reason for not sharing that little tidbit of information, Lily didn't look forward to tiptoeing around Brendan Kane for the next two weeks.

The man had no sense of humor.

She'd tried to tease him. Tried to get him to lighten up a little and make the best out of an uncomfortable situation. But her attempt had been met with silence. Oh, and another frown.

At least they didn't have to share the same living space, although Lily suspected that working in close proximity would prove to be difficult enough.

From the brief conversation they'd had in the office the day before, she could tell there were no boundaries between Brendan's professional life and personal life. He was ambitious. Single-minded. Devoted to his career.

Lily recognized the signs. A few weeks ago, she'd been the same way. But watching your best friend battle fatigue and constant pain had a way of changing a person's perspective. Made her see what was really important.

Thank You, God.

It was a prayer Lily had repeated at least a dozen times every day.

The cell phone on the nightstand chirped, starting a countdown to Brendan's arrival. He'd claimed he was in the office by seven in the morning, so Lily had set her alarm for six.

She dashed down the hall to shower and then slipped into her uniform—paint-splattered overalls and a clean T-shirt—before making her way downstairs to the kitchen. Even though Sonia had given her permission to raid the refrigerator, Lily didn't want to take advantage of her host's generosity. She planned to drive into Castle Falls later that afternoon and pick up a few things at the grocery store.

She did, however, locate the coffeemaker and brew a fresh pot.

During her brief tour of the house the day before, Lily had discovered a stone patio located off the back of the kitchen. She shouldered open the weathered screen door and stepped outside, a steaming mug of coffee in one hand and her Bible in the other.

Proof that her morning routine had changed, too. A few months ago, Lily's definition of "time with God" had been a muttered prayer, asking God to bless her day, as she sprinted to her car. Never realizing that a continued conversation with God, the privilege of sharing her heart, *was* the blessing.

She lowered herself into a wicker rocking chair that faced the river and closed her eyes, letting the scents and sounds wash over her as she thanked God for the beauty of His creation.

When she opened them again, she was no longer alone.

A dog with long ears and an even longer body sat next to the chair, staring up at her with liquid brown eyes.

Lily smiled at her unexpected visitor. "Well, good morning. Where did you come from?"

Sonia hadn't mentioned owning a pet, but Lily couldn't quite picture Brendan choosing this particular breed to be his canine companion. Although it *would* explain the mournful expression on the basset hound's face. And its sausage-like shape? Evidence of a master who practically lived in his office.

Lily took pity on the poor thing.

"You can hang out with me for a while. How about that?"

The dog's tail thumped the ground, which Lily interpreted as a yes. She tucked the Bible under her arm and the basset hound trotted alongside Lily as she made her way back to the house.

With limited access to Brendan's office, she'd decided to concentrate on the living room. By the end of the day, the glowing tangerine walls would be replaced with a soft shade of aqua. Pale. Serene. A respite from a stressful day.

Lily had a feeling she would be spending a lot of time there.

"First things first." Lily looped a bandanna around her hair and knotted the ends together at the nape of her neck. "In this line of work, it's function over fashion."

The basset hound made a strange sound.

Lily glanced down and saw a colorful piece of cloth clamped in her jaws.

She laughed.

"I guess this means you want to help."

Chapter Three

Laughter.

It was the first thing Brendan heard when he opened the front door the next morning.

That's all he needed. Someone in the house holding a paintbrush in one hand and a cell phone in the other.

Brendan bypassed the kitchen, ignoring the lure of freshly brewed coffee as he strode down the hall to the living room. If he and Lily Michaels were going to be sharing space for the next two weeks, it wouldn't hurt to establish a few ground rules. Let her know what he expected…

He pulled up short in the doorway.

Lily was kneeling in front of the fireplace. The paint-splattered overalls she wore somehow managed to enhance her slender curves rather than detract from them. Two bright golden tassels peeked out from underneath the green bandanna tied around her head.

No paintbrush. No cell phone. Instead, she was holding on to the corner of another bandanna… the other end was attached to an overweight basset hound.

It couldn't be.

"Missy?"

Brendan realized he'd said the word out loud when Lily's head jerked up.

"Is that your dog's name?" Smiling at him, she surrendered the colorful strip of fabric.

"She's *not* my dog."

Missy clattered over to him and deposited the damp cloth at his feet.

"Really?" Lily rose to her feet and parked her hands on her hips, a pointed look at Missy conveying her skepticism.

"My mother volunteers at the shelter and she tries to find people willing to adopt the animals that end up there." Although Brendan had no idea how the dog had covered the mile-long trek from town on those stubby little legs.

"She's a stray?"

"Not anymore," Brendan said quickly. "Mom found a home for her before she left. Missy must have gotten loose somehow and wandered away."

There was also the distinct possibility she'd been dropped off on his front porch in the middle of the night.

"Maybe she thinks *this* is home." Lily looked down at the basset hound, and her expression softened.

The furry martyr collapsed at his feet with a heavy sigh.

Brendan inwardly rolled his eyes. "I'll give Mr. Wilson a call and let him know Missy's here."

"She's probably thirsty." Lily moved past him and the scent of her shampoo, something light and citrusy, teased his senses. "I'll get her some water."

"There's a dish under the sink." Brendan pivoted in the opposite direction and retreated to his office to find a phone book. He was expecting a call from a customer within the next few minutes and a shipment of materials for their next order was on its way, something Brendan needed to sign for when it arrived.

He punched in Ed Wilson's number, foot tapping the floor in time with every ring. Just before he was about to hang up, Brendan heard a click.

"Wilson residence."

"Mr. Wilson? This is Brendan Kane. I'm calling because you must have—" *give the man the benefit of the doubt now* "—misplaced something. Missy showed up here a little while ago."

"So that's where she ran off to." Brendan heard a rusty chuckle. "All I can say is the good Lord must have put a homing device in those critters when He created them."

"Her home is with you," Brendan reminded him.

"Can't keep her," Ed said bluntly. "My son called last night and invited me to spend the summer in

Chicago, but he lives in one of them fancy condos. No pets allowed."

"I understand." Brendan squeezed the base of his skull, a futile attempt to ward off the tension headache snaking its way up the back of his neck, one vertebra at a time. "Thanks for your time, Mr. Wilson."

"Sorry I can't help you out."

Not as sorry as Brendan.

The second call he made was to the animal shelter. It rang ten…twelve times…before Yvonne Delfield answered with a breathless hello. The woman was a close friend of Sunni's, one of the few who'd actually supported her decision to take in three rowdy boys who'd slipped between the cracks of the child welfare system.

"Missy is with me," he said without preamble.

"Brendan?" And then, "Oh, that's a relief! I was hoping you'd decided to keep her."

"What? No, I didn't…. July is one of the busiest months of the year." Brendan put Yvonne on speakerphone and fired up his computer to confirm the time of an afternoon appointment. "She managed to escape from Ed Wilson and ended up back here. I was just calling to make sure someone would be around when I bring her back to the shelter."

"Oh." The word rolled out with Yvonne's sigh. "One of the county deputies found a litter of puppies living in a shed and brought them in, so we're a little short on space at the moment. Would you be willing to keep Missy until Sunni gets back and finds another home for her?"

"No problem."

Brendan heard the words, but he hadn't *said* them.

He pivoted toward the doorway, and his gaze locked on Lily. Her wide smile didn't hold the least bit of repentance for eavesdropping on a private conversation. Missy sat at her feet, and it looked as if *she* was smiling, too.

If Brendan hadn't known for a fact that, at that very moment, his mother was sunbathing on the promenade deck, he would have accused her of orchestrating the whole thing.

Lily finished rinsing out her paintbrush and turned off the faucet in the laundry room sink. A few yards away, Missy dozed in a patch of afternoon sunlight streaming through the blinds, paws pedaling the air as she chased a phantom squirrel in her dreams.

She couldn't help but smile as she remembered Brendan's reaction to her impulsive announcement to provide a temporary home for the dog. She hadn't meant to eavesdrop, but a deliveryman had shown up at the front door with an invoice that needed Brendan's signature. She'd arrived just in time to hear a woman asking him to keep the dog until Sunni returned.

Guessing what the answer would be, Lily had squeezed in a yes before Brendan could say no.

Honestly, how could the man even consider returning Missy to the shelter when he had plenty of space for a dog to roam?

A question she'd asked after he'd hung up the phone.

Brendan had taken the clipboard from her outstretched hand, walked out the door and tossed one word over his shoulder.

Trouble.

Lily begged to differ. From what she'd witnessed so far, the dog was proving to be far more agreeable than its master.

Brendan hadn't been exaggerating about the amount of time he spent in his office. Their paths had intersected once in front of the coffeepot, but other than that, the door to his office had remained firmly closed the rest of the morning.

Lily plucked a towel from a hook on the wall next to the sink and dried off her hands.

"I don't know about you, Missy, but I'm getting hungry. What do you think about lunch?"

Judging from the speed with which the dog rolled to her feet, she must have thought it was a pretty good idea. Missy followed her to the kitchen and watched Lily raid the refrigerator.

A quick inventory of the contents yielded the ingredients for a fairly presentable Cobb salad. While the eggs boiled, Lily diced up a thick slice of smoked ham and shredded a pungent wedge of Wisconsin cheddar to sprinkle on the top of the fresh greens.

After laying everything in a pretty glass bowl, she stepped back to admire her work.

Plenty for two.

Lily yanked out that thought before it could take root.

No. Way.

Brendan had made it clear he didn't want any interruptions.

Until God had gotten her attention, Lily been the same way. She'd turned down so many invitations from her coworkers to join them in the employee lounge for lunch, they'd finally stopped asking.

Lily felt an internal nudge and groaned.

Really, Lord? Because I'm pretty sure the man keeps a box of thumbtacks stashed in his desk drawer in case he gets hungry.

Another nudge.

And because Lily had made a promise she would never ignore those divine promptings again, she took a deep breath and rapped on the door of Brendan's office.

"It's me. Lily," she added unnecessarily.

She waited. And waited some more. Just when she was about to give up, the door swung open and Lily found herself face-to-face with a…wall of blue denim. Lily was by no means petite, but she was forced to tip her head back to meet Brendan's gaze.

"Five minutes," he growled.

"Five minutes," Lily mused, refusing to be intimidated by The Frown. "Five minutes to pack my bags and get out of Dodge? Five minutes for the police to arrive and arrest me for trespassing? I'm afraid you'll have to be more specific."

"Four minutes and fifty-eight seconds." He wasn't closing the door when he said it, though, which gave Lily the courage to follow through with her mission.

"I wasn't sure what your plans were for lunch—"

"I usually eat in my office."

Alone.

Even though he didn't say the word out loud, it flashed like a blue neon sign in his eyes.

Oh, well. She was halfway up the hill. Lily decided there was no point in retreating now.

"It's a beautiful day to soak up some sunshine and the beautiful view." *The view you can't appreciate because your desk faces the wall.* "You could eat outside at the picnic table."

From the expression on Brendan's face, Lily would have thought she'd asked him to participate in some unfamiliar—and slightly disturbing—ritual.

"Sunni put you up to this, didn't she?"

"Up to what?"

"Lunch. Sunshine."

Lily grinned. "You make them sound like health hazards."

Brendan took a step back, as if *she* were the health hazard. "I can't today, but…thanks. I'll grab something later."

"All right." She shouldn't have been surprised. "I'll put half the salad in a container for you. I used up the rest of Sunni's salad dressing, but I can pick up a bottle when I go to the grocery store later this afternoon."

Lily knew she was chattering. Brendan didn't care about salad or salad dressing. What she didn't know—and what she was afraid to analyze too closely—was the pinch of disappointment she'd felt when he'd turned down her invitation.

Brendan glanced down at Missy, who'd bravely camped at her feet during their brief exchange. "I have an appointment with a client, so I won't be able to keep an eye on the dog."

"That's all right, I'll bring her along." Lily reached down and fondled one of Missy's silky ears. "She's been a perfect companion all morning. I don't know why you called her trouble."

Suddenly, there it was again. The shooting star of a smile that had had Lily's stomach performing backflips the day before.

"Who said I was talking about Missy?"

The door snapped shut.

Brendan stepped onto the patio and felt a stab of unease.

The evening breeze stirred shadows into the river, turning the water from sapphire to a deep indigo.

After Lily had returned from the grocery store, he'd watched her disappear into the woods, a colorful backpack slung over one slim shoulder and Missy trotting along at her heels.

They should have been back by now.

Had Lily decided to hike up to the falls? Alone?

The path along the river wasn't well marked, although Brendan could have found it in the dark. He and his brothers had explored every inch of these woods when they were kids.

If you'd had lunch with Lily, maybe she would have told you her plans.

Brendan tried to shake the thought away but it stuck to his conscience like a burr on a wool sock.

It had been self-preservation, pure and simple. There was no doubt in his mind that Sunni had had an ulterior motive when she'd hired Lily.

Mom thinks you're lonely.

Once again, Aiden's words cycled through his mind.

It wasn't that Brendan was anti-relationships. He just knew the successful ones took time and attention—and right now, the business required all of his. He'd been talking to the CEO of Extreme Adventures for several months and, finally, it looked as though his persistence was paying off. Filling orders for the sporting-goods chain guaranteed stability in a competitive market and uncertain economy.

Brendan should have realized that Sunni hadn't given up her matchmaking, she'd simply changed tactics. His mother knew the long hours he spent in the office weren't exactly conducive to getting to know the single women living in Castle Falls, so she'd *imported* one.

Although why Sunni thought he'd be attracted to someone like Lily Michaels was a mystery. The woman was too stubborn. Too...perky.

Too distracting.

The fact that he was in front of the window instead of his computer screen proved it.

Unfortunately, Lily was also running out of daylight.

Which meant it was up to him to make sure her and her furry sidekick made it safely back to the house.

Brendan grabbed a flashlight from a shelf in the hall closet on his way out the door. The moon was already rising over the trees, and adrenaline spiked Brendan's blood as he picked his way along the narrow foot path that ran parallel to the river. If Lily was on her way back, he should have met up with her by now.

He hiked another quarter mile, judging the distance by the subtle change in the river's current. Castle Falls was just up ahead, an appropriate name for the steep sandstone wall that towered above the water.

"Lily?" Brendan pitched his voice a notch above the rushing water. In the fading light, he spotted the trunk of a dead aspen near the base of the falls. The jagged stub of a branch had caught on one of the rocks, holding the tree in place as it bobbed gently in the foam.

Like a suspension bridge.

Brendan's breath snagged in his lungs even as he tried to rein in his overactive imagination. The challenge of crossing the river on a *stick* might prove irresistible to his two younger brothers, but a grown woman would be too level-headed to attempt it....

"Hi!"

He twisted toward the lilting voice and saw Lily waving to him from the opposite side of the riverbank.

Apparently not.

Stubborn. Perky. Now Brendan could add reckless to the list he'd started.

"It's so beautiful here!" Lily skipped across the fallen tree with the nimbleness of a professional tightrope walker.

Halfway across, the log shifted, and Brendan heard her gasp.

Without thinking, he splashed into the shallow water, shoes and all, and reached for her.

"Thanks." Lily latched on to his hand, and the warmth of her touch shot up his arm like a current of electricity.

Brendan sucked in a breath and let her go the moment their feet touched dry land. "What—" he tossed the word down like a gauntlet "—did you think you were doing?"

Lily smiled up at him, eyes shining in spite of the fact she'd almost fallen into the river. "Exploring, of course."

Of course.

Brendan shook his head. "Look, the sun is setting—"

"I know! I watched it from up there." She pointed to one of the granite turrets that bracketed the water spilling over the top of the falls. "The best seat in the house."

The best seat... Brendan tried to shut down the image what could have happened if Lily had lost her footing and slipped. Or somehow stumbled upon the cave located behind the falls.

Brendan battled the temptation to share the discovery he'd made years ago. To watch her face light up with wonder.

Now who's the reckless one?

"You probably spend a lot of time here." Lily clapped her hands and Missy trundled out of the brush, sporting a brand-new collar that could have only been purchased in the pet food aisle of the grocery store.

"No." Spotty cell phone reception and no internet equaled no customers. "Not really."

"You should." Lily cast one more longing look at the falls before she fell into step beside him.

Brendan didn't answer.

There were a lot of things he knew he *should* do.

Spending time with Lily Michaels definitely wasn't one of them.

Chapter Four

Lily's gaze bounced from the gleaming, freshly primed wall to her laptop, where a perky woman wearing a pristine white smock was demonstrating a cutting-edge technique in the world of faux finishes. She made it look so easy. But then again, *that* painter didn't have to contend with a neighbor who didn't want her to listen to the radio. Or sing along with it. At one point, when Lily had started a pleasant, albeit one-sided conversation with Missy, the heels of Brendan's chair scraping against the floor on the other side of the living room wall let her know that he didn't want to hear anything at all.

Absolute silence might have been Brendan Kane's idea of a perfect work environment, but it was driving Lily bonkers. Listening to music while she worked helped her stay on task. And she could use a little focus—especially when the only thing she *could* hear was the husky—and rather appealing—

rumble of a masculine voice on the opposite side of the wall every time the telephone rang.

And it rang a lot.

"You'll want to work quickly before the base coat dries," Perky Painter was saying. "Then, wait thirty minutes! Plenty of time to grab a fresh cup of coffee or take a little walk and stretch your legs."

Missy, who'd been napping in the corner, lifted her head at the word *walk*.

"Later," Lily promised. Because, while she'd been tuned into Brendan's rich-as-dark-chocolate tenor on the other side of the wall, the base coat *had* started to dry.

She tapped the rewind button on the DVD player and followed the directions, ignoring the pull and protest of unused muscles while she worked. Who would have guessed that painting could take the place of a daily workout? No wonder Shelby didn't bother with a gym membership.

A red-winged blackbird landed on a low branch just outside the open window and trilled a greeting. Lily responded with a series of whistles that sounded, in her opinion, like a fairly decent imitation of the bird's cheerful dialogue.

A floorboard creaked. The door at the end of the hall snapped shut. Was Brendan taking an unscheduled coffee break? Or had he added whistling to his own personal neighborhood-watch list?

The steady tread of footsteps drew closer.

Watch list.

"I'll distract him while you make a break for it," Lily told the bird. She felt a pinch of envy when it took wing and disappeared into a hedge of golden spirea. The only cover available for her was the drop cloth that now doubled as a dog bed.

While Lily contemplated how long it would take to displace the basset hound and dive underneath it, Brendan appeared in the doorway.

He looked frazzled. And grim. Two things that should have canceled out the "and handsome" part of the equation. But—Lily tried not to sigh—they didn't.

When Brendan had shown up at the falls the evening before, she'd been ridiculously glad to see him. Not because the sun had retreated, allowing shadows to fill the spaces between the trees while she'd been exploring, but because the man had finally ventured out of his office.

Apparently the only thing that separated Brendan from his routine was something that disrupted it.

And that something would be you, Lily.

As someone who'd had to rewind the video tutorial—twice—since she'd started working, she decided they were even.

"The delivery truck has a flat tire a few miles from town so I'm going to round up a spare and drive it over," Brendan said. "I'm expecting an important call, so I'll be back in half an hour or so."

"All right."

Lily tried to sound casual, but the sudden glint in

Brendan's eyes meant he'd seen the hopeful glance she'd sneaked at Sonia's radio, a charming relic from the 1970s that resembled a toaster and boasted real dials instead of a touch pad.

"You'll have plenty of time to bang a few pots and pans together." Brendan's dry statement could only be a reference to Lily's brief foray into the kitchen, when she'd whipped up a veggie omelet for breakfast. "Sing. Tap dance. Make all the noise you want."

Cheering, Lily thought. That would be the noise she'd be making.

Brendan's lips twitched. That he'd read her mind was as unnerving as the possibility a real live heart beat underneath the pocket of his black polo.

Lily was relieved when Missy rolled to her feet, spotted her reluctant host and released a joyful howl.

He winced. "You're still here."

Lily imagined Brendan had thought the same thing a few hours ago, only he wouldn't have been referring to the basset hound.

"Where else would she be?"

"In the kitchen, chewing on a table leg? Hunting for shoes to bury underneath the hostas?"

At least now Lily knew where to look for her missing flip-flop.

Not deterred by Brendan's less than flattering assumptions, Missy shuffled toward him, tail wagging.

"I'll be back." Brendan ducked out of the room before the basset hound could shed on his khakis.

Lily smiled down at her. "You just earned that walk."

The phone rang while Lily was in the kitchen, mixing up a fresh pitcher of iced tea. Brendan still hadn't returned, although it had been well over an hour since he'd driven away to assist the truck driver. The ringing stopped, only to start up again less than a minute later.

Brendan had said the call was important....

She dashed down the hall to his office and reached for the phone. "Good morning! Castle Falls Outfitters."

"Who is this?" The question wielded a suspicious edge, as if the caller knew someone else should have answered the phone.

"Lily Michaels. I'm—"

"The painter Sunni hired to give her house a makeover! She told us all about it the book club meeting last week." The caller's tone warmed several degrees. "She didn't mention you'd be helping Brendan out in the office, too."

"I'm not." Lily wondered what the woman would say if she confessed the man had banished her from that particular room. "Brendan had to step out for a few minutes, but I'd be happy to take a message."

"I'd appreciate that! This is Jill Robinson, and I'm calling to remind Brendan about the picnic the soccer team is hosting on Tuesday."

Lily reached for a pen to jot down the details. "Soccer picnic. Tuesday."

"This is the first year the kids at New Life Fellowship formed a team," Jill chatted on. "The booster club parents host a picnic at the beginning of the season to thank the businesses that provide funding for our equipment and uniforms. Brendan agreed to sponsor the Conquerors."

"That's great." So great that Lily might be forced to reevaluate her first impression of the man. "What time?"

"Four o'clock in the field right behind the church." Jill paused. "By the way, our Sunday morning worship service starts at ten if you're interested in attending tomorrow."

"I'd love to." Lily meant it. Church attendance was one of the things she'd added during the recent but major restructure of her life.

"My husband and I will be manning the coffee station in the foyer, so be sure to stop by and say hello."

"I will. And I'll pass this information onto Brendan as soon as he gets back," Lily promised. "He was looking forward to your call."

"He…" Jill had a sudden coughing fit. "Really?"

"Of course." Lily drew a smiley face next to the information, ridiculously pleased to discover that Brendan did occasionally venture out of his office.

"I can't wait to meet you, Lily." Jill chuckled. "You certainly seem up for a challenge."

"It's not so bad." Lily eyed the algae-green walls. "All the place needs is a little updating."

"Oh, I wasn't talking about the house, honey."

Lily was still pondering what Jill could have meant when she hung up the phone.

Brendan strode up the sidewalk, one hour and thirty-eight minutes later than he'd planned.

The trucking company had no business hiring people who didn't have a clue how to change a flat tire. But then again, the guy he'd found sprawled on the hood, tethered to his iPod by a bright orange cord dangling from one ear, didn't even look old enough to hold a valid driver's license. Brendan had ended up changing the tire and unloading the cargo into his own vehicle.

Just to make sure it didn't end up somewhere in Canada.

The house was eerily quiet when he opened the front door.

No humming. No whistling. Lily must have taken his polite request for peace and quiet to heart.

It was bad enough the lower half of the house now resembled the paint aisle of a home-improvement store, but on his way to check something in the shop earlier that morning, Brendan happened to glance into the living room. Lily had been stretched out on the rug in front of the fireplace, reading the label on a plastic tub with the intensity of a law student studying to pass the bar exam. Missy was sprawled across her legs, her whiskered chin resting on Lily's knee.

Two thoughts had collided in Brendan's mind. Lily looked as if she belonged there. And, for the first time, he'd wished he could trade places with a dog.

Halfway to his office, the tantalizing aroma of cinnamon beckoned to him from the kitchen. Brendan took a deep breath, determined to forge ahead…

"Hi." Lily landed in front of him, looking like a sunbeam in the yellow apron he'd bought for Sunni one Christmas.

Bare toes, each one painted a bright shade of coral, peeked out from the rolled up hems of Lily's faded jeans. "I was starting to get a little worried."

Brendan was getting a little worried, too. Worried that it didn't matter if Lily sang along with the oldies on his mother's ancient AM/FM radio. Or kept up a lively dialogue with Missy.

Her very presence in the house had somehow changed things.

"The driver didn't know how to change a flat." Brendan noticed a smudge of grease on the back of his hand and took a quick detour over to the sink. "You didn't happen to hear the phone ring, did you?"

"Yes…and I also happened to answer it." Lily fished a piece of paper from the pocket of Sunni's apron, embroidered with the words *Hug the Cook*. Somehow, the words took on a whole new meaning.

Don't. Go. There.

Brendan plucked the paper from Lily's hand and glanced at the name scrawled at the top. "Jill?"

"Robinson." Lily grabbed a potholder and opened the oven door a crack. A burst of steam rolled out, carrying the scent of apples. "One of the parents in the booster club."

"What booster club?"

"For your soccer team."

"I don't *have* a soccer team."

"New Life Fellowship. The Conquerors." Lily's sigh stirred a wisp of hair on her forehead. "Does that ring a bell?"

"No—" Okay. Maybe a very *faint* one.

Lily tipped her head. "You hear it, don't you?"

In spite of his rising frustration, Brendan battled a sudden urge to smile.

"Jill said that Castle Fall Outfitters—your business—is sponsoring the team."

The pieces were beginning to come together. "I signed a check."

"Hence the word *sponsor*." Lily fisted her hands on her slender hips. "You said you were expecting her call."

"I said I was expecting an *important* call," Brendan shot back. From Garrett Bridges, the CEO of Extreme Adventures.

"It sounded important to Jill."

"Was that the only time you heard the phone ring?" Brendan had been in contact with Bridges often enough over the past few months to know that he and the CEO were a lot alike. Every minute of the day attached to a certain task. If something disrupted the flow or severed the connection, they didn't have time to wait around. They simply moved on to the next thing on their agenda.

"It might have. I took Missy for a walk right after Jill called." The flash of guilt on Lily's face made *him* feel guilty. It wasn't her responsibility to answer his phone. She'd done it as a favor, even though he'd enforced a code of silence all morning. Never mind that Lily had kept breaking it.

Or that he'd looked *forward* to her breaking it.

"Don't—" Worry about it, Brendan had been about to say. But a series of short, staccato barks peppered the air, shooting holes in his apology.

Lily's gaze locked on something outside the window. "Hold that thought."

The screen door slapped shut behind her as she charged outside.

Brendan didn't want to know what kind of trouble Missy had gotten into. Again. As he contemplated who might benefit from the responsibility of taking care of a pet—Aiden instantly came to mind—he heard another door slam.

"Something smells good!"

Brendan froze when his brothers sauntered into the kitchen.

"What are you doing here?"

Aiden shoulder-bumped Liam. "Told you he missed us."

"We decided to come back a day early." Liam's nose lifted like a timber wolf's on the hunt. "Do I smell apple pie?"

"I have no idea," Brendan said irritably. "Did something go wrong? Did you run into bad weather? Was there a problem with the new design?"

Liam ignored him. "You don't know what's in the oven?"

"I don't know because I didn't make it," Brendan muttered. "Lily Michaels did."

"Who is Lily Michaels?" Aiden wanted to know.

"The painter Mom hired, remember?" Liam hunkered down and peered through the oven door for a better look.

Aiden turned to stare at him. "You're letting her use the kitchen?"

"Not exactly." Brendan wasn't *letting* Lily do anything. She'd invaded his home…his territory…at his mother's invitation and there was nothing he could do about it. Just like there was no sense hiding the fact the arrangement included room and board. Liam and Aiden would figure it out soon enough. "Mom let her move into the guest room. Temporarily," he added, more for himself than his brothers.

That pulled Liam's attention away from the oven. "She's staying here?"

"Yes." Brendan bit down on the word. "Her business is based in Traverse City, and it's too far to commute every day."

"Why didn't Mom hire someone local?"

"I have no idea." Even though he was afraid that he did.

Sonia assured me that I have all the qualifications she's been looking for.

Brendan wasn't about to confess that he was afraid Sunni's commitment to finding a companion for him had risen to a whole new level.

"Oh, oh. I know that look." Amusement danced in Aiden's eyes. "Lily Michaels is getting in your way, isn't she?"

Getting in his way. Under his skin.

"She's only been here a day," Brendan snapped.

His brothers exchanged a knowing look.

"She's one of those drill sergeant types who wants to take over," Liam guessed.

"Kind of sounds like someone else we know." Aiden grinned. "No wonder you look like you drank a glass of river water— Whoa!" He jumped back as Missy streaked past him, tail slashing the air like a windshield wiper set on high. Scattering drops of water on everything—and everyone—in her path.

"Sorry!" Lily was right behind the dog, pink-cheeked and breathless. "Missy spotted a trout in the shallow water and decided to do a little fishing…." The violet eyes widened when she realized he wasn't alone. "Hello."

Brendan suppressed a groan.

Because Liam and Aiden were looking at Lily the way Adam must have looked when God introduced him to Eve in the garden.

* * *

Handsome in triplicate.

It was the only way Lily could describe the wall of ruggedly handsome, dark-haired men standing in the kitchen. Three pairs of eyes, in shades of watercolor hues ranging from the translucent blue of an April sky to cobalt, were locked on her.

Brendan had mentioned his brothers in passing the day before, but even if Lily had formed a picture in her mind, her imagination still wouldn't have done them justice. Like Brendan, the two newcomers topped six feet and boasted the lean but muscular build of a quarterback. Skin stained a deep golden-brown by the sun testified to the number of hours they spent outdoors.

One of them flashed an engaging smile as he stepped forward. "Liam Kane."

"Lily Michaels. It's nice to meet you." Lily wondered if she sounded as bemused as she felt.

Brother number two stepped forward and extended his hand. "Aiden. And if that apple pie tastes as good as it smells, I might have to find a few more things to paint around here so you'll stay longer."

Lily took the blatant hint as a compliment and laughed.

"You're certainly welcome to try it. There's plenty." She reached for a potholder on the counter but Aiden beat her to it.

"I've got it."

Brendan's eyes narrowed. "Don't you two have a trailer to unload?"

"The canoes aren't going anywhere. But this..." Aiden winked at Lily as he removed the steaming pie from the oven and set it on the counter. "Well, I wouldn't want it to disappear while I'm gone."

Brendan snorted. Because some men clearly didn't appreciate good food when it was delivered right to their office door.

Liam bent down to pet Missy, who sat patiently at his feet, a puddle of river water expanding around her as she waited to be noticed. "I thought Mom found a new home for her."

"Ed Wilson couldn't keep her, and the shelter didn't have room," Brendan said.

"You're going soft on us, big brother," Aiden teased.

"Don't look at me." Brendan crossed his arms and looked at *her.*

"I...intervened," Lily admitted.

"Interfered," Brendan said under his breath.

Whatever the term, it was obvious *someone* hadn't gotten over it yet.

Lily grabbed a roll of paper towel from the counter as tiny tributaries began to fan out from the puddle underneath Missy and channel into the grout between the ceramic tiles.

"How did you get Bren to agree to let her stay?" Liam asked, eyes lit with curiosity. "He told us Missy was chewing him out of house and home."

Lily hesitated. Was this a trick question? "Um...I just told him I would take care of Missy until Sonia came home."

"Just told him, huh?"

Brendan's brothers exchanged a smile. And a look that Lily couldn't quite interpret.

"Mom *has* been on a mission lately." Liam propped a hip against the table and glanced at Brendan. "What's that verse she likes to quote?"

Lily, who'd never been blessed with siblings, sensed a subtle change in the atmosphere. The kind of weighted stillness that usually precedes a thunderstorm.

"I can't remember," Brendan said tightly.

"I do." Aiden's smile flashed. *"It's not good for man to be alone."*

Liam burst out laughing, and Aiden joined in.

Brendan didn't.

As much as the Kane men looked alike, Lily had just discovered one characteristic that distinguished Brendan from his brothers.

His disposition.

Chapter Five

Brendan didn't know which brother to muzzle first.

He'd been hoping Liam and Aiden wouldn't figure out why Sunni had hired a self-described "custom" painter. A painter who lacked so much confidence in her ability she had to watch a tutorial before starting a project.

Brendan had caught a glimpse of a woman wielding a paintbrush on an open laptop, but it was the guilty look on Lily's face right before she'd snapped it shut that caught his attention. He suspected his mother hadn't even bothered to check Lily's references before she'd signed the contract.

Because she had all the qualifications Sunni was looking for...

"I'll help you unpack." Brendan took a step toward the door.

No one followed.

"So what do you think of Castle Falls, Lily?" Aiden yanked a clean plate from the dish drainer.

"Have you had a chance to get acquainted with the area yet?"

Brendan could see where this was going, and it made the decision easier.

His youngest brother first.

"Mom hired Lily to paint, not go sightseeing," Brendan reminded him.

"I plan to do both, actually." Lily smiled. At his brother. "The area is beautiful."

"You should hike up the river when you get a chance." Liam nudged Aiden aside and began to rummage through the utensil drawer for a fork. "The falls are kind of a well-kept secret around here because they're located on private property and not in a state park."

"Who owns the land?" Lily opened the freezer and pulled out a container of vanilla ice cream Brendan hadn't known was there.

The situation was quickly getting out of hand. Not only had Lily staked a claim on the living room, she'd invaded Sunni's kitchen and stocked it with contraband. His brothers would be circling the table all day if she kept this up.

"We do," Aiden said. "And—"

"She's already been there." Once again, Brendan relived the moment he'd seen Lily blithely skipping across a fallen log while the current did its best to shake her loose. And once again, the cartilage in his knees turned to mush at the thought of her getting pulled beneath the surface of the churning water.

Aiden, of course, ignored him. "What did you think of the cave?"

Lily tipped her head in a gesture that was becoming as familiar to Brendan as her bright smile. "Cave?"

"You didn't tell her about the cave?" His brothers turned and launched a verbal strike at the same time.

"I didn't think about it." The truth was, Brendan didn't *want* to think about it. A memory shivered through him, as cold as the water that trickled down the amber walls of the cave they were discussing.

"He didn't say anything about a cave. And I didn't see it when I was exploring," Lily said.

"It's not near the falls...it's *behind* them." Without missing a beat, Aiden broke a pact the three of them had made years ago. For the second time. "Brendan discovered it when we were kids."

"You have to go through a passageway to get to it, though," Liam added.

"It's kind of dark and creepy, too," Aiden put in cheerfully.

Most women would have been deterred by that information. If possible, Lily appeared even more intrigued. Brendan was beginning to realize that Lily Michaels couldn't be lumped in the category of "most women."

For the first time since his brothers had wandered into the kitchen unannounced, Lily made eye contact with him. "That must have been a great place to play."

Or hide.

A memory began to work its way to the surface and Brendan thrust it back down again. Some things were better left in the past.

"Yeah." Liam slanted a look at him. "Ready to unload that trailer now, big brother?"

"Sure." Brendan wasn't sure whether to be relieved or annoyed that he hadn't masked his reaction to Lily's innocent comment as well as he'd thought he had. But then again, Liam had always been the most intuitive one in the family.

Aiden reluctantly set the plate down.

"It has to cool a little before I can cut it anyway." Lily must have seen the look of disappointment that crossed his youngest brother's face. "But you're welcome to come back and try a piece when you're finished with your work."

"Count me in." Liam clapped Brendan on the shoulder. "I'll eat Brendan's piece, too. He doesn't take a break until ten o'clock at night."

Why bother to deny it? "I still have a few phone calls to make." Even if the thought of leaving Lily alone with his brothers made Brendan feel as if he was wearing a wool shirt inside out.

Half an hour later, after dodging portage packs and barrel bags and the smug looks tossed his way, Brendan retreated to his office to tackle the next thing on his agenda.

Thirty seconds later, there was a soft tap on the door.

"Come in."

Given the fact that Liam thumped the door with his fist like he was trying to put a dent in it and Aiden didn't bother to knock at all, by process of elimination, Brendan wasn't surprised when the door swung open and Lily poked her head inside the office.

What *was* a surprise was the way Brendan's heart kicked against his rib cage when she smiled at him.

"I brought you a piece of pie."

"Thanks." Brendan flicked a glance at the plate in her hands. "You can just set it aside in the kitchen, though. I don't have time to eat it right now."

"Are you sure about that?" Lily rocked forward on her toes and nodded at the calendar on his desk.

"What..." Brendan glanced down. In a narrow space between his two and three o'clock phone calls, someone—and there was no question who that someone was—had written the words *apple pie*.

In permanent marker.

"Enjoy." She set the plate down and was gone before he could summon a protest.

Clearly, Lily Michaels had no respect for boundaries.

Brendan sighed as he reached for the fork.

"There's *three* of them?"

"Uh-huh." Lily kept the phone pressed to her ear as she jogged to keep up with Missy, who'd veered off the gravel driveway and begun to blaze a new trail through the woods.

The dog had risen with the sun and in her eagerness to start the day, she'd made sure Lily was up and ready to start hers, too.

"I've been in the custom-painting business for three years, and most of my clients are older women who are diehard fans of HGTV," Shelby complained. "How did you manage to get bachelors number one, two and three?"

"Sonia hired me," Lily reminded her. "Her sons just kind of…came with the place."

"OASHA would approve," Shelby teased. "What a great work environment."

Except for the "silence is golden" rule that Brendan had been so quick to enforce. But it was so good to hear her friend laugh again, Lily decided not to argue that particular point.

"Aiden and Liam live in an apartment above the garage and spend most of the day in the shop. I doubt I'll see much of them."

"What about the other one? Brendan? What does he do?"

"He—" *Bosses people around? Drives her crazy?* "—manages the business side of things."

"Does he know you're in marketing?"

Lily almost dropped the phone. *"No."*

"Why not?" Shelby demanded. "You're amazing!"

Under different circumstances, Shelby's staunch loyalty would have made Lily smile.

"I'm not in Castle Falls to drum up new business," Lily reminded her. "I'm here to help with yours. Besides that, Brendan Kane isn't crazy about someone invading his turf. I'm pretty sure if he found out I'm an amateur, it wouldn't matter that Sonia was the one who'd signed the contract. He would fire me first and ask questions later."

"It isn't like you don't know what you're doing," Shelby huffed. "You helped out once in a while when we were on summer vacation."

"I stirred the paint and put tape around the windows."

"Well, you're a fast learner and can do anything you set your mind to."

"Tell that to my father," Lily joked.

Shelby, the friend who was privy to her deepest secrets and knew her better than anyone else, didn't laugh. "I'm sorry he gave you a rough time about taking a leave of absence from Pinnacle. I should have figured out another way to keep things running until I'm back on my feet."

"Don't worry." The last thing Lily wanted to do was add to her friend's burden. Shelby needed to concentrate on getting well. "My job will still be there when I get back."

Along with a promotion and a corner office, if her boss kept his promise.

"That doesn't sound like the Lily Michaels who refused to leave her lemonade stand unattended so she could spend her afternoons by the pool." Shelby chuckled. "Although, come to think of it, you were the only kid in our neighborhood who could afford a new bicycle that summer."

A bicycle Lily had taught herself to ride.

Absently, she traced the moon-shaped scar on her elbow, evidence of a run-in with Mrs. Gillespie's mailbox. "Someone once told me that a person can't see the big picture when their nose is pressed against the grindstone."

"That sounds like a very wise woman...who happens to be envious of *your* view at the moment."

Lily heard an undercurrent of wistfulness flowing below the words and sent up a silent but fervent prayer for her friend's continued healing. It had been weeks since Shelby had felt well enough to venture more than a few feet beyond the living room sofa.

"When I get back, we'll spend a whole day in your garden, pulling weeds and planting...stuff." Lily wasn't a gardener, unless, of course, the shriveled cactus in her kitchen window counted as a houseplant, but Shelby loved being up to elbows in fresh dirt.

"That sounds wonderful." Her friend sighed. "And in the meantime, I'll be praying for you. God has you in Castle Falls for a reason, you know."

"Um...I'm pretty sure I'm here because of you." Lily teased, knowing Shelby had always appreciated a sense of humor over a show of sympathy. "Or maybe the Lord knew Missy needed someone to take care of her."

Shelby snickered. "Or her owner."

"Trust me, Brendan Kane doesn't want anyone taking care of him." The leftover Cobb salad in the refrigerator proved it.

"What makes you think I was talking about Brendan?"

"I—" Lily's heart stuttered. Because Mr. I-Don't-Share-My-Office-with-Anyone should have been the last Kane brother who came to mind.

"I'll give you some time to think about it." Shelby was still laughing when she hung up the phone.

Lily didn't want to think about it. She didn't even want to think about *why* she didn't want to think about him. *It.*

Slipping her cell into the pocket of her skirt, she scanned the woods for her four-legged friend.

In the past twenty-four hours, Lily had discovered the basset hound's favorite pastime was finding things—to chew on or roll in.

"Missy!" As she ducked under branches and skipped over roots protruding from the ground, Lily ruefully acknowledged the trees were winning. She'd decided to take Jill Robinson up on her invitation to attend the service at New Life Fellowship that morning, but she would be late if she didn't leave within the next few minutes.

When she came to the back of a familiar building, Lily realized she'd been led in a gigantic circle. Parked on a strip of gravel between the shop and a weathered cabin was a hunter-green pickup truck.

Missy sat in the driver's seat.

"Oh, no. No. *No.*" Lily was beginning to think Missy's name was a shortened form of Mischievous. "You can't be in there!"

Missy obligingly hopped over the middle console and landed on passenger seat.

"Hey! I called shotgun."

Lily started at the sound of a masculine voice and then released a sigh of relief when she realized it was Aiden who'd turned up at the scene of the crime.

"She jumped in through the window." Lily silently measured the distance from the ground to the cab of the truck and frowned. "Just don't ask me how."

"Come on, Missy." Aiden opened the passenger-side door and tried to coax her out.

"Looks like we've got a stowaway."

Liam suddenly materialized at her side and Lily felt a stab of sympathy for the women in Castle Falls. Both of Brendan's brothers had upgraded from yesterday's faded jeans and lightweight flannel to khakis and button-down shirts that accentuated their broad shoulders. Lily also couldn't help but notice these men were *smiling* at her, too. A comforting change, to say the least.

But that didn't stop her from looking past them, trying to see...

The one you don't want to see, remember?

"Lily?"

Guilt lit a fire in Lily's cheeks when she realized she hadn't responded to Liam's comment. Hopefully he would assume her blush stemmed from losing Missy and not her sanity.

"Sorry." Lily forced a smile. "I guess I should have bought Missy a leash to match her collar."

"Don't worry about it," Liam said. "She didn't hurt anything."

"Speak for yourself." Aiden laughed as he staggered away from the truck, weighed down by forty pounds of wriggling basset hound. He tried—unsuccessfully—to avoid the swipe of Missy's tongue against his cheek as he set her down on the ground. "Take it easy now."

"And people claim dogs are good judges of character," Liam murmured.

"What can I say?" Aiden's blue eyes danced with mischief. "The ladies can't seem to resist my charm."

Liam rolled his eyes. "Your blarney, you mean."

Listening to their banter, Lily found herself wishing that Brendan was as easygoing and uncomplicated as his brothers. Any fears she'd had about Liam and Aiden resenting her presence in the house had been put to rest the day before when they'd invited her to join them for a piece of pie and then peppered her with questions about her plans for the house.

Laughter had punctuated their lively conversation and Lily could tell that even the good-natured insults flying back and forth across the table welled from a deep affection rather than malice.

She couldn't help but compare it to the rare times

her father had actually been home for the evening meal. She'd told Shelby once that their interaction was more like dinner interrogation than conversation. Her father expected a list of things Lily had accomplished that day followed by the goals she'd set for the next.

Gaining his approval had become Lily's ultimate goal. Until she'd realized it was an unreachable one. She swept the thought aside, along with the feelings of regret that inevitably accompanied it.

"Those short little legs sure don't slow her down much." Liam pointed to Missy, who'd set off after a monarch butterfly that drifted past.

"Or stop her from breaking into unattended vehicles." Lily sighed. "I promise I'll keep a closer eye on her."

"No harm, no foul," Liam said easily.

"Especially when the unattended vehicle belongs to Brendan, not us," Aiden added with a grin.

Now Lily was *really* sorry.

"I'd better take Missy back to the house so I can make it to church on time." *And disappear before Brendan made an appearance.*

Aiden's gaze bounced from her to Liam and back again, a smile brewing in his eyes. "Which one?"

"New Life Fellowship."

"So are we," he said cheerfully. "You're welcome to ride with us."

"I don't want you to go to any trouble."

"It's only two miles down the road, and we're

going to the same place," Liam said. "I don't call that trouble."

Lily doubted Brendan would have the same perspective. But Liam hadn't mentioned that his older brother would be attending the service with them....

"All right." She gave in.

"We'll swing by the house and pick you up in five minutes," Aiden said.

Lily lured Missy to the door with a biscuit she'd stashed in her pocket and closed her in the three-season room once they were inside. The wicker furniture provided the least amount of temptation for a dog who viewed leather furniture as a gigantic rawhide chew.

A short time later, a sleek black convertible—not a pickup truck—pulled up in front of the house with Aiden at the wheel. Lily slung her purse over her shoulder and glanced at her reflection in the oval mirror hanging in the hallway. Cheeks flushed pink from chasing Missy through the woods. Hair loose around her shoulders instead of confined in a tidy French braid.

Oh, well. It was a good thing God looked at the heart!

Lily locked the door and skipped down the steps. Liam hopped out and opened the car door the moment before she reached it.

Smiling, Lily slid inside. "Thank—"

The rest of the sentence stuttered and died when her gaze locked on the man sitting in the backseat.

Hair gleaming like obsidian from a recent shower, Brendan wore dove-gray dress pants that accentuated his long legs and a white linen button-down shirt.

She almost didn't recognize him.

Brendan was staring at her as if he didn't recognize her, either. And then he frowned, which, Lily thought ruefully, proved that he had.

Chapter Six

"Good morning."

Lily fanned her skirt over her knees and tossed a quick smile in Brendan's direction, ridiculously pleased to discover he took time away from work to attend church on Sunday morning. Even though it was a little unsettling that he was going to be attending with *her.*

"Morning." Brendan practically grunted the word.

Lily suspected he left out the "good" part of good morning on purpose. An awkward silence swelled between them as she fumbled with her seat belt.

I'm trying, Lord, I really am. But I could use a little help.

One of the verses in a Psalm Lily had read during her devotional time that morning came to mind and she latched on to it like a lifeline.

This is the day the Lord has made, let us rejoice and be glad in it.

Rejoice. Be glad.

Lily turned toward the window, pulled in a slow breath and let the words take root in her heart. There were plenty of things to rejoice about. Birds singing in the trees. Sunlight streaming through the canopy of trees that bowed over the road. The sky a deep velvet blue, the same shade of blue as Brendan's eyes....

"Careful!"

Liam rasped out the warning a split second before Aiden swerved to avoid a rusty chunk of metal in the road. Lily gripped the leather seat in order to avoid ending up in her seatmate's lap.

"That was close," Aiden said cheerfully.

Lily couldn't argue with the statement. Her silent promise to appreciate God's blessings didn't *include* Brendan Kane. Or the blue eyes she'd vowed not to think about.

"We are now approaching Riverside Avenue." Aiden put on his best tour guide voice as they reached the city limits. He turned onto a narrow street. "Any guess as to how it got its name?"

Lily tapped her finger against her lips and pretended to think about it. "Because it runs alongside the river?"

"Gold star for Lily Michaels."

Brendan shook his head. "You missed the turn."

"I thought Lily might appreciate the scenic tour of Castle Falls."

Liam twisted around in his seat and smiled at her.

"We won't be late for church. It only adds a whole thirty seconds to the trip."

"Scenic sounds great." With Missy in the car, Lily hadn't had an opportunity to explore Castle Falls during her brief excursion to the grocery store the day before.

On one side of the river, the town was laid out in a tidy grid, each of the side streets connected to Riverside Avenue like bicycle spokes. Wicker baskets overflowing with red geraniums and trailing ivy swung from the brass lampposts stationed like sentinels on every corner. The car continued down Riverside, where Lily counted a hardware store, the bank and a bakery. A freestanding chalkboard stationed in front of the plate-glass window listed the pies being sold that day.

"Just ahead, on your left, is Castle Falls' answer to social networking." Aiden pointed to a storefront in the middle of the block, and Lily couldn't help but smile.

The brick had been whitewashed and splashed with black polka dots all the way up to the wrought-iron balcony on the second floor. Bistro tables in a rainbow of colors lined the sidewalk on both sides of the carnation-pink door that marked the entrance.

Lily read the sign on the marquee and chuckled. "The Happy Cow?"

"Best frozen custard this side of the Mackinac Bridge,"

Liam said, "On a hot summer day, the line of

customers stretches all the way down the street and around the block. You can't find a place to park on Riverside."

"Unless you happen to be in a canoe. There's a spot you can land it fifty feet from the back door." Aiden's eyes met hers in the rearview mirror and he winked. "I'm speaking hypothetically of course. Because that would give someone an unfair advantage."

"It would also interfere with *someone's* work day," Brendan said drily.

It shouldn't have come as a surprise to Lily that Brendan's first contribution to the conversation had something to do with work.

"I think it's important to explore the local points of interest." She shot a challenging look in his direction. "I'll be sure to add it to my list."

"You have a list?" Brendan's raised eyebrow challenged her right back.

Only because old habits die hard, Lily thought. But this list happened to be a new and improved version of the one she stored in her iPhone. It included more than appointments and notes about upcoming projects and deadlines. It included, well…life.

"If I were you, I'd pencil in a visit on Tuesday," Liam was saying.

"*Triple-Scoop* Tuesday," Aiden corrected his brother. "For the price of a single cone. There are thirty-six flavors on the menu, but the Kane brothers would be more than happy to accompany you and offer their expert advice."

Brendan was already shaking his head. Lily felt a stab of disappointment. In that moment, Brendan reminded her of her father, who took pride in the fact he hadn't taken a day of vacation in twenty years. Even while Lily's mother was alive, becoming a partner in his law firm was all he'd cared about. The title engraved underneath his name, the measuring stick of his success.

"Sorry, The Happy Cow isn't on my calendar." Brendan slid a look at her. "At least it wasn't the last time I looked."

His tone didn't change but there was *something*.... Lily blinked, convinced she'd imagined the smile teasing the corner of his lips. A smile she found more fascinating—and infinitely sweeter—than an ice-cream shop on Castle Falls' main street.

Their eyes met and held. The space between them seemed to shrink, and Lily felt a little like Alice when she'd stepped through the looking glass. Trying to make sense of emotions as confusing to her as the unfamiliar territory in which Alice had found herself.

She couldn't be *attracted* to Brendan. Could she?

No, she couldn't. He had his priorities, and work was at the top of the list. Her father had been the same way, sacrificing relationships for promotions. Taking business trips instead of vacations.

Lily didn't want that kind of life. Not anymore.

"Last stop on today's tour," Aiden's voice broke into her thoughts. "New Life Fellowship church."

Brendan lifted one eyebrow, and Lily yanked her gaze away, wishing she could blame the sudden redness on her cheeks on the sunlight shimmering against the window.

She turned her attention to a stately brick building at the very end of a quiet residential street. Stained-glass windows absorbed the early morning sunlight, and double oak doors were propped wide open, welcoming people inside. The steeple looked as if it had been hewn from one of the ancient oaks that created a natural fence between the church and an open field beyond the parking lot.

Aiden braked for a young couple who'd just gotten out of a minivan. Four little girls in white eyelet sundresses trailed behind them, hand in hand, linked together like a string of pearls.

"So, what do you think of Castle Falls?" Liam asked as Aiden found an empty parking space in the shade.

"It looks more like a movie set than a real town." Lily smiled. "You must have loved growing up here."

Her comment was met with absolute silence. Even Aiden, her irrepressible tour guide, didn't say anything.

Liam cleared his throat. "We—"

"Are going to be late." Brendan finished the sentence.

Lily dared a glance at him. The smile she might

have imagined, but not the shadows that chased through his eyes.

Tour or not, it was clear some things were strictly off-limits.

Brendan rose to his feet as the notes of the last hymn faded.

He made a point never to linger after the Sunday morning worship service. Although he'd attended New Life Fellowship since high school, every time he shook someone's hand, he still felt as if his character were being weighed and measured. And found lacking.

You must have loved growing up here.

Lily's innocent comment had slipped through his defenses.

Pierced the wall Brendan had built around his heart. People tended to have long memories, and Brendan had gotten himself into more than a few scrapes when he and his brothers had moved to Castle Falls.

"Good to see you, Brendan."

Speaking of scrapes, one of them was blocking his path now. Although to the man's credit, Seth Tamblin seemed to have forgotten it was his locker that had borne the brunt of Brendan's temper after fourth-period gym class one afternoon.

"Pastor." Brendan extended his hand.

"I'm glad you invited Lily Michaels to the service this morning." Seth's hairline might have receded since their sophomore year of high school but his gap-toothed grin remained the same. "Your mother wanted to make sure she got to know some people while she's here. Rebecca is hoping she can convince Lily to join the women's book club on Friday morning."

Brendan shouldn't have been surprised the pastor knew Lily's name and where she was staying. Apparently his mother had shared that information with everyone.

Everyone but *him,* anyway.

"Lily won't be in Castle Falls very long," Brendan pointed out. "Sunni hired her to paint a few rooms in the house. It's only a temporary position."

Emphasis on the temporary. Not long enough to join a book club. Not long enough to explore the woods. Not long enough to pose any significant threat to his schedule.

Or his heart.

"No matter how long a person stays in Castle Falls, we want to make them feel at home." Seth cuffed Brendan on the shoulder, a gesture he wouldn't have dared to attempt when they were teens.

Before Brendan could tell the pastor that wasn't a problem for Lily—she'd already made herself at home—the pastor excused himself and moved on to greet another member of the congregation.

Brendan continued down the center aisle, fielding the curious looks with a polite smile because he knew they weren't directed at him. Even with the stream of summer tourists passing through town, a newcomer was guaranteed to draw attention.

Especially one as stunning as Lily.

When Liam had said they needed to make a quick stop on the way to church, Brendan hadn't thought much of it.

Until the front door opened and he hadn't been able to think at all.

Instead of baggy overalls spattered with paint, Lily wore a sundress scattered with blue flowers that accentuated her slender waist and flared over the curve of her hips. The braids were gone, freeing a mane of golden-blond hair that captured the sunlight and danced around her shoulders.

Brendan had barely been able to suppress a groan when Lily slid into the backseat and invaded his space. Aiden and Liam, on the other hand, didn't seem to mind that their mother had installed a stranger in the house during her absence. To Brendan's acute frustration, his brothers seemed as determined to seek out Lily's company as he was to avoid it.

Brendan made his way past the coffee station. Not even the aroma of freshly ground beans tempted him to linger as he pulled out his cell phone to check his voice mail. Garrett Bridges still hadn't called to talk about the new contract, and the delay was making Brendan uneasy. True, it was Sunday, but to guys like the CEO of Extreme Adventures, seven days, not five, made up a typical workweek.

"Hi, Mr. Kane!"

A hedge of kids wearing blue-and-white jerseys suddenly sprouted in front of the doors, forcing Brendan to pull up short to keep from mowing them down.

"Excuse me." He stepped to the side and tried to advance again, but the line shifted and blocked his path.

"Brendan! I've been looking all over for you."

A woman who looked vaguely familiar bustled over and held out her hand. "Jill Robinson. I don't think we've officially met before, but Sunni is a good friend of mine."

Ninety percent of the population of Castle Falls could make the same claim, Brendan thought wryly. And even though he didn't know Jill Robinson, his mother probably knew the woman's middle name, birthday and favorite flavor of ice cream. Sunni had grown up in the town, graduated salutatorian from Emerson High School and the following summer, two days after her eighteenth birthday, she and Rich Mason had exchanged vows in this very church.

In a small town, that kind of history practically guaranteed a front row seat at the Fourth of July parade.

Brendan had lived in Castle Falls for fifteen years, and he was still considered an outsider. Not that he'd ever made an attempt to rectify the situation.

"Sunni is still on vacation." Brendan couldn't think of another reason why she would waylay him.

"And having a blast, I'm sure." Jill grinned. "On behalf of the soccer club parents, I just wanted you to know how much we appreciate your sponsorship…and to show off the new uniforms. They just came in yesterday!"

On cue, the group of munchkins spun around and presented their backs to Brendan. The words Castle Falls Outfitters had been silk-screened on every jersey in enormous block letters.

"It's not a big deal." In fact, his mother was the one who'd suggested it.

"It is to the team." Jill beamed at the children as they turned around to face him again. "And we're all thrilled you agreed to attend the picnic on Tuesday."

Brendan narrowed his eyes. "What picnic?"

"The soccer picnic. Didn't Lily tell you that I called?"

"Yes." But she hadn't mentioned anything about a picnic.

Over Jill's shoulder, Brendan spotted Lily standing with Rebecca Tamblin, the pastor's wife, laughing together as if they'd been friends for years. "Will you please excuse me for a minute?"

"Sure," Jill sang out. "We'll be setting up under the trees next to the parking lot. See you then!"

Brendan dodged the clusters of smiling people. Because at the moment, there was only one smiling person he wanted to talk to.

"Lily?"

She whirled around at the sound of his voice and

coffee sloshed dangerously close to the rim of her cup. "Is something wrong?"

"I just spoke with Jill Robinson?"

Lily's brow furrowed, as if she wasn't quite sure why he'd phrased it as a question. "She's the one who called about the picnic."

"I remember the phone call," Brendan said softly. "But I don't recall you mentioning that I was invited."

"She said the soccer club hosts one at the beginning of the season to thank the businesses who sponsor a team."

"But…" Brendan left the word dangling like a clue until understanding dawned in her eyes.

"That doesn't mean you planned to *attend* the picnic," Lily guessed.

"Right." He lobbed the word back at her.

"Why not? It'll be fun."

"Fun," Brendan repeated.

"Something that provides amusement or enjoyment? You must be familiar with the word."

"I have things to do." Even if Brendan couldn't remember what those things were at the moment. Not when Lily's teasing smile dared him to see the humor in the situation. "Not everyone can afford to fritter away an evening." Disappointment doused the sparkle in her violet-blue eyes.

"I'm sorry."

Why did he get the impression Lily wasn't apologizing for the misunderstanding?

"Look—" Brendan felt a tug on his sleeve. He glanced down...and down a little farther...then blinked to make sure he wasn't seeing double. Two little girls about seven or eight years old were grinning up at him, the blue-and-white jerseys that hung to their knees as identical as their freckled faces. Only one family in Castle Falls boasted hair the color of a newly minted penny.

"Anna Leighton's girls?" Brendan guessed.

"We're Conquerors!" The twins slapped their palms together. "Go Conquerors!"

Brendan winced. The look he shot Lily questioned her definition of the word *fun.*

Well, there was a lot the man didn't know.

Lily bent down until she and the girls were eye to eye.

"Great team spirit. I'm Lily by the way."

"I'm Cassie, and I'm the goalie." Pride flashed in the girl's amber eyes. "Chloe is a forward. Mrs. Robinson said to tell you that you don't have to bring anything to the picnic 'cause you're the guest of honor."

"Unless you want to. 'Cause the hot dogs are always kind of *burnt,*" Chloe confessed in a whisper.

Cassie nudged her twin. "But we get Popsicles for dessert."

"Popsicles are wonderful on a hot summer day." Lily heard Brendan snort and the sound reminded her of a bull getting ready to charge.

"You can have one, too," Chloe offered. "There's lots."

Lily wasn't sure how to turn down such a sweet invitation.

But something told her that she should put some space between her and the man standing beside her. As quickly as possible.

"I—"

"We thought you two had left without us." Brendan's brothers suddenly appeared at her side.

Relief coasted through Lily that Liam and Aiden had inadvertently come to her rescue.

"Beat you to the donuts!" Giggling, Cassie and Chloe scampered away.

Slack-jawed, Aiden and Liam watched the girls join their teammates in front of the refreshment table.

"What's the matter?" Brendan said irritably. "You two are acting like you've never seen little kids before."

"It's not that." Liam scratched the back of his head. "I don't think we've ever seen you *talking* to little kids before."

Lily ducked her head to hide a smile.

Brendan rolled his eyes. "The soccer club is hosting a picnic for the businesses that sponsor a team, okay?"

Aiden's eyes widened a fraction as the meaning sank in. "We sponsor a team? No kidding."

"When's the first game?" Liam wanted to know. "Maybe we can cheer them on."

"The sponsors aren't obligated to attend the

games." Brendan frowned and then pierced her with another look. "Are we?"

"I have no idea," Lily said sweetly. "You're the sponsor."

Lily suddenly realized that Brendan's brothers were staring at her in bemusement, their expressions identical to the one they'd had on their faces when they'd found their brother deep in conversation with the two pint-size soccer players.

"You and Aiden could attend the picnic in my place," Brendan said suddenly. "I'm sure no one would mind."

"I don't know about that." Liam grinned. "Like Lily said, you're the sponsor."

Chapter Seven

Lily finished rinsing out her paintbrushes and tipped her face toward the sky. The gray clouds that had dispensed an early morning shower had been chased away by the sun and promised a beautiful evening.

Perfect for a picnic.

Lily couldn't help but smile. She was sure Brendan was hoping the gentle rain would have turned into a monsoon that canceled Tuesday's event.

She hoped he hadn't changed his mind. The team had looked so proud of their new jerseys. Lily found their excitement contagious, but judging from Liam and Aiden's reaction to the news that Brendan had sponsored the soccer team, it seemed he'd had built up an immunity to anything that would take him away from work.

"Are you taking a break or are you done for the day?"

Lily turned to smile at Liam—and realized he

wasn't alone. Brendan stood beside his brother and Lily felt her heart give a funny little kick.

"Done," she decided. "The paint has to dry until tomorrow morning."

"Aiden and I are going out on the river for a couple of hours." Liam didn't seem to notice Brendan's frown. "Would you like to join us?"

"That sounds like fun." Lily took a step forward, but a large hand snagged her elbow.

Brendan's hand.

"She can't," Brendan interrupted. "She's busy."

"Busy?" Lily swallowed hard.

"You're coming with me to the picnic."

A jolt of heat radiated up Lily's arm and spread directly to her heart, which immediately picked up speed. Her mouth went dry but she somehow managed to scrape up two simple words.

"I am?"

"It wouldn't be fair for you to miss out on all the… fun." Brendan unleashed a slow smile in her direction. One that changed the landscape of his chiseled features and spilled over into his eyes.

Fair?

Lily swallowed hard. She could tell *him* something else that wasn't fair. Both Liam and Aiden Kane were drop-dead gorgeous. But when they smiled at her, there wasn't a single flutter or shiver. No clammy palms or weak knees. So why did one of Brendan's smiles make her feel as if she were riding the Tilt-A-Whirl at the county fair?

"Missy is going to need a walk." Lily latched on to what she thought would be the perfect excuse.

"I can do it," Aiden volunteered.

For the first time, Lily wished Brendan's brothers weren't so nice.

"I—" she tried to come up with an excuse and failed "—guess I'll see you later."

Brendan released her elbow, and Lily was finally able to release the breath she'd been holding. Until his fingers fanned out against the small of her back.

"We don't want to be late."

Once again, Lily was unable to piece together a coherent thought, let alone a protest.

By the time she and Brendan arrived at the church, a large group of people had already gathered around tables set up under the maple trees.

Jill, who was stationed at the end of the serving line, waved a set of tongs at them. "Don't be shy! There are plenty of hot dogs left."

"Of course there are." Brendan peeled back a corner of tin foil covering the serving dish and warily eyed the charred main entrée.

"Think of it this way," Lily whispered. "It's not safe to eat undercooked meat."

Brendan lowered his head and his breath stirred a wisp of hair over her ear. "I don't think whatever this is qualifies as meat."

A shiver danced down Lily's spine, and she lurched from the line, sidestepping the teenager handing out snack-sized bags of potato chips. Barbecue flavor, which happened to be her favorite kind. Sometimes, Lily told herself, sacrifices had to be made for the greater good. At the moment, the greater good meant putting some space between her and the man wreaking havoc with all the switches and wires connected to her heart.

And remembering why she'd come to Castle Falls—and how long she planned to stay there.

God brought you to Castle Falls for a reason.

Lily swallowed a sigh. Why did Shelby's little gems of wisdom always pop into her thoughts at the most inopportune times?

Because there was one thing she knew for sure: Brendan Kane wasn't—couldn't be—part of a divine plan. If anything, he was one of the obstacles in her path. The man practically *camped* in his office from dawn to dusk, making it difficult for her to get inside and do the prep work needed before the room received its scheduled makeover.

Several people waved and smiled, but Brendan bypassed the crowded tables and chose an empty one at the far end of the picnic area instead. Lily had no choice but to follow.

Was he still upset he'd had to shorten his work day? Or was something else going on? Lily couldn't help but notice that while most of the people had lingered in the large foyer after the worship service on Sunday morning, laughing and catching up on each other's lives, Brendan had made a beeline for the door immediately after it ended.

"How long have you been attending New Life Fellowship?"

Lily swapped her dill pickle for a handful of his potato chips.

Brendan's gaze slid away from her. "Fourteen... fifteen years."

Lily tried to hide her astonishment. If that were the case, she would have expected Brendan to be on a first-name basis with most of the people in the congregation, especially given its size.

"Everyone seems friendly," she ventured.

Brendan didn't respond as he dug into the mound of potato salad on his plate.

Okay, *almost* everyone.

She took the hint and lifted her face to the sun, feeling its warmth as she closed her eyes. "It's a perfect summer evening, isn't it?"

Perfect.

Brendan shifted his gaze from Lily's profile. The delicate fan of golden lashes against her cheeks. The curve of her lips...

He closed *his* eyes.

What was he doing here?

He'd planned to update the homepage of the business website and get a jump on his to-do list for the week. But here he was, surrounded by a pack of kids running laps around the picnic tables, fueled by red sports drinks. The majority of their parents were the people Brendan had managed to keep a polite distance from since high school.

Until Lily intervened.

He glanced at her, a picture of contentment as she munched on a charcoaled hot dog and sipped lukewarm lemonade from a paper cup. She didn't look dangerous, but the mischief that lurked at the edges of her smile warned Brendan not to let his guard down.

"Finished?" He rose to his feet and chucked his paper plate into a nearby trash can. When he turned, he came face-to-face with the two freckled-faced copper tops who'd been assigned to capture him in the church parking lot. "Thank you for the…food… and good luck when you play your first game."

"You can't leave yet, Mr. Kane!" Chloe, or was it Cassie, grabbed one of his hands.

"Why not?" He balked when her sister grabbed the other one and tugged. "Where are we going?"

"You have to watch our game," Cassie said.

"Game?" He looked at Lily.

"I didn't know anything about a game." She traced an invisible X on her chest. "Promise."

Brendan wasn't sure whether to believe her or not, but the Leighton twins were already towing him toward the field, so he didn't have an opportunity to question her further.

A group of adults were setting up folding chairs, their red T-shirts and caps matched the jerseys of the children doing warm-up exercises on the grass. Their coach, a stocky man with iron-gray hair, circled the team, clipboard in hand as he barked out commands.

"That's the Raiders," Cassie said. "They're really good."

"One of my friends played them last year, and she said they kick," Chloe chimed in.

"That's how you play soccer," Brendan said.

"Not the ball," Chloe whispered. *"People."*

"Hard." Cassie cast a nervous glance at the players in red.

Lily, already a diehard Conquerors fan, looped her arms around the girls' thin shoulders and gave them a bracing squeeze. "Just do your best and have fun, okay?"

Brendan shook his head. There was that word again.

"Okay!" Boosted by the pep talk, the twins bumped their fists together and ran onto the field.

Brendan moved toward a row of empty chairs set up on the sidelines, but Jill Robinson bounded over and cut him off.

"Oh, no, you don't!" She pointed to a spot farther down the field where a group of parents wearing blue-and-white were handing out water bottles. "We have a special place for our guest of honor."

Brendan followed the invisible line until he landed on that "special place." Out of the corner of his eye, he saw Lily double over and pretend to tie her shoe. When she straightened again, the only smile that remained was in her eyes.

"The kids set it up," Jill informed him proudly.

"I'm—"

"Honored," Lily said under her breath.

"Speechless." Brendan could ad lib when the situation called for it.

"That's not all!" As enthusiastic as a game show host, Jill pressed a blue-and-white shirt and a matching ball cap into his hands. "The team had the jersey made especially for you."

"That's so thoughtful," Lily said. "Isn't it, Brendan?"

"Thoughtful." And, judging from the width of the shoulders, two sizes too big.

"We didn't forget you." Jill turned to Lily and gave her a hat. And two blue-and-white pom-poms. "You are now an official Conquerors cheerleader."

"Mrs. Robinson?" A boy waved at her from the sidelines.

"Where's the first-aid kit?"

"Gotta run!" Jill dashed away, leaving Brendan holding a jersey emblazoned with the words *Number One Sponsor* on the back.

"Do I really have to wear this?"

Lily was already twisting her hair into a silky rope and threading it through the hole in the back of her ball cap. Her smile tipped in his direction.

"We can trade."

"No, thanks." A jersey for pom-poms? He'd have to throw in his man card, too.

Lily gave the pom-poms an enthusiastic shake. "Let's see some Conqueror pride."

"I didn't realize that was a prerequisite when I signed the check."

"Think of it as an unexpected bonus. Like the jersey."

Lily patted his arm. "I realize it means shifting from high gear into neutral for a little while, but you can do it."

Brendan wasn't sure about that. Neutral meant resting and he wasn't particularly good at that. Not when there was so much at stake. The future of the company. The family's livelihood.

The fulfillment of a promise he'd made.

The reminder sent him running for cover—away from Lily's infectious grin and the satin-smooth touch of her hand. Even if the only refuge available happened to be a chair shaded by an umbrella large enough to shade a small country.

Up close, the thing was even gaudier than Brendan had thought. "Why does this feel more like a punishment?"

"You have a cup holder." Lily wagged a finger over her head. "And an umbrella—with tassels."

"Yeah. Thanks for pointing that out."

The mischievous twinkle in Lily's violet eyes came out to play. "You're welcome."

Brendan wrestled with a smile and lost.

Lily sucked in a breath.

Really, those unexpected smiles should be accompanied with some kind of warning so a girl had time to batten down her emotional hatches.

She hooked her foot around the metal leg of her spindly chair and pulled it out of the shadow cast by the oversize umbrella shading Brendan's chair. Better a little sunburn than the kind of heat generated by one of his smiles. Until she'd fallen under its spell again, Lily hadn't realized she'd been patiently waiting for another sighting.

"Hey, Mr. Kane." A lanky teenage boy loped up to them and stuck out his hand. "Josiah Aldridge. Mrs. Robinson said I should come over and introduce myself."

"You look a little older than the rest of team," Brendan observed.

"That's because I'm the coach." Josiah appeared less than thrilled by the idea. "Perry, my older brother, was supposed to be here, but he broke his ankle waterskiing a few days ago. Three pins."

Lily cringed at the thought. "That's terrible."

"The last time it was four," Josiah said, way too cheerfully in Lily's opinion. "Perry is sort of accident prone. I guess it's a good thing our mom is a nurse."

Brendan frowned. "But you play soccer, right?"

"Nope. The guitar." Josiah shrugged. "But how hard can it be? All you have to do is kick the ball between the goal posts, right?"

"In the net," Brendan muttered.

"Whatever." Josiah shrugged. "Gotta go. My friends are coming over for a jam session in my garage in an hour." Josiah strummed an invisible guitar as he jogged backward onto the field. "Time to beat the Rangers."

"The Raiders," Lily said. But the teenager was already out of earshot.

Brendan was shaking his head.

"What's wrong?" Lily was almost afraid to ask.

"A game usually runs an hour and a half." Brendan leaned back in the chair. "So unless the coach is planning to take off at halftime, his band is going to be short a guitar player."

"He wouldn't do that." Lily nibbled on her lower lip. "Would he?"

"I doubt it." Unfortunately, Brendan didn't sound too sure.

Leaning forward, Lily scanned the field and saw another potential problem. "Isn't there some kind of an age range separating each division? The Conquerors look six inches shorter than the Raiders."

"I have no idea. I just—"

Signed the check.

Lily silently filled in the blank when Brendan's cell phone began to shriek for attention. He glanced at the screen and vaulted to his feet.

"Excuse me."

"Sure…" Brendan was already walking away. The purposeful stride and set of his shoulders told her the call was business related.

Lily doubted there was anything truly pressing that required Brendan's attention on a Tuesday evening, but it was almost as if he were afraid to relax.

She'd been the same way. Striving to achieve the next goal, Lily had missed out on the good stuff. Making dinner instead of ordering takeout. Having a real conversation with Shelby instead of shooting off a quick text message or email between deadlines.

She wished someone would have encouraged her to balance her schedule more, to make room for the things that were really important, but Pinnacle rewarded the employees who clocked the most hours, generated the most sales…

Lily felt that little nudge again. The one she was beginning to think should be accompanied by the theme song from *Mission Impossible*.

Oh, no, Lord. Absolutely not. I tried that once. Remember the salad?

All the reasons why Brendan Kane was *not* the kind of guy who would appreciate a take-time-to-smell-the-roses pep talk began streaming live through Lily's head.

Number one, the man has a chronic case of tunnel vision.

Number two, he thinks I'm neglecting my job when I take Missy outside for a walk. And let's not forget that he would rather sign a check than volunteer his time....

Lily's gaze shifted from the game to the man standing alone near one of the picnic tables. Even from the distance that separated them, she could tell there was something wrong.

Lily closed her eyes.

Okay, I'll try. That's the best I can do, Lord. The rest is up to You.

Chapter Eight

"I'm really sorry, Brendan. At least my clients don't expect Castle Fall Outfitters to return their deposit."

Brendan's hand tightened around the phone. He resisted the urge to tell the Realtor he couldn't return the money even if he wanted to. They'd used it to purchase the supplies necessary to fill the order. "Are you sure they don't need a little more time? This thing has been in the works for quite a while, hasn't it?"

"Five months." A sigh unfurled on the other end of the line. "Unfortunately, it's dead in the water… no pun intended. They're out."

They weren't the only ones, Brendan thought.

In the spring, a local Realtor had contacted him on behalf of three couples from Chicago that had decided to purchase a condominium together. Now, less than a week before the final paperwork was signed, the Realtor's clients had had a falling out, and the deal was off. Which meant Castle Falls Outfitters just lost an order for six recreational canoes in the space of a ten-second phone call. Brendan figured that had to be some kind of record.

It also proved how much they needed the Extreme Adventures contract. It wasn't the first time a customer had canceled an order, but the income from the canoes would have gone a long way to cushion the decline in sales that inevitably coincided with a long winter.

The thought of breaking the news to his brothers left Brendan with a sour taste in his mouth. The last time he'd checked with Liam, he and Aiden had already devoted dozens of hours to the project and were currently finishing the fourth canoe. The one person Brendan *wouldn't* tell right away was their mother. It had taken weeks to convince Sunni to accept the cruise they'd booked for her birthday. If she found out they'd lost an order that size, Brendan knew the guilt would shadow the memories of her vacation like a little black rain cloud.

"I hope we can do business together in the future," the Realtor was saying.

Brendan murmured a polite response even though the chance of another order that size was slim. Right before he slipped the phone in his pocket he saw he had a new voice mail waiting. At some point between the charred hot dogs and getting settled under the tasseled umbrella, he'd missed a call. He tapped in the password and heard Garrett Bridges's voice.

"I'm at the airport..."

Brendan's back teeth snapped together as he listened to the rest of the message. He wanted assurance the contract was in the mail, not a curt update from the CEO informing Brendan he planned to be out of the country until the end of the week but there were a few more things he "wanted to discuss."

Another delay.

Brendan felt as if he'd been sucker punched. Twice. He'd been doing everything in his power to prove Castle Falls Outfitters could handle a major expansion, but for some reason, Bridges continued to drag his feet.

Brendan glanced at the time the call had come in and debated whether he should return it. A noisy soccer field wasn't exactly the ideal environment to hold an important conversation, but Brendan decided to take a chance the CEO was still sitting at the gate and not in first class.

On the fourth ring, he heard a click, followed by a cheerful automated response. *"You have reached the voice mail of Garrett Bridges..."*

Frustration sluiced through Brendan's veins as a robotic voice advised him to leave his name and number and a brief message. He wouldn't have missed the call if he'd been in his office. There were no kids there. No picnic lunches. No soccer games.

No Lily.

As if she felt his gaze, Lily turned around and waved.

Her smile alone tempted Brendan to forget the

future of the family business rested squarely on his shoulders.

Further proof that Lily was the most dangerous distraction of all.

A shrill beep pierced Brendan's ear, a reminder it was time to leave a message. Five seconds after he hung up the phone, Brendan received an incoming call from Garrett Bridges. "Where are you?" the CEO barked. "I left a message almost half an hour ago and the flight attendant is threatening to take my phone away. Isn't this why I pay for first class?"

A cheer erupted and Brendan turned toward the field. Lily was on her feet, pom-poms shaking. Brendan wrestled down a smile. Did she realize the Raiders had scored the goal?

The other spectators must have wondered the same thing, because heads began to swing in her direction. Oblivious of the attention, Lily broke into a fancy little shuffle that made Brendan wonder if she *had* been a cheerleader in high school.

Her impromptu sideline dance produced the desired effect because the kids perked up like Sunni's petunias after a warm summer rain.

"What's that racket?" Garrett growled. "Are you at the circus or something?"

Or something.

Brendan battled another smile. "Not exactly. What can I do for you?"

"I have a three-hour layover at Heathrow tonight,"

Bridges growled. "I'll call you from the airport. Are you planning to answer your phone this time?"

Brendan didn't miss the barely veiled sarcasm as he calculated the time difference in his head. Not that it would have made any difference. He'd stay awake all night if necessary. "I'll be available."

"Good. Marketing has a few concerns they wanted me to bring to your attention." A click ended the call.

Brendan resisted the urge to hit redial and demand more details. How many more obstacles did he have to contend with?

It had taken several months of negotiations to convince Bridges that a small, family-owned business could provide the amount of inventory necessary to stock the large stores in the sporting goods chain. Marketing hadn't come up in prior conversations with the CEO. What specific concerns was Bridges talking about?

The possibilities began to stack up as Brendan made his way back to Lily's side.

"Bad news?" She twisted in her chair to look at him.

"Why?" Brendan hedged.

"Oh, I don't know." Lily tipped her head and pretended to consider the question. "Your shoulders are tense, and if you squeeze that cell phone any harder, the battery is going to pop out." Her hand settled over his, linking them together. The warmth of her skin almost made Brendan forget about the canceled order...the subtle warning from Garrett

Bridges hinting that Brendan could lose the contract. Just about everything.

Something he couldn't afford to do. With the Extreme Adventures contract stalled in the negotiation process, now wasn't the time to lose his focus.

"I'm fine."

Still, it was more difficult than Brendan imagined it would be to let go of Lily's hand.

What was she thinking?

Lily knotted her hands in her lap to make them behave. It was more difficult to steady the erratic beating of her heart.

She reminded herself that Brendan didn't want— or appreciate—what he no doubt considered interference. The man didn't even want her in his office. What made her think he would appreciate her asking questions?

Or holding his hand?

The referee blew the whistle, and the Conquerors trudged off the field, their faces flushed red from shame rather than exertion as they lined up for a water break. Josiah took advantage of a brief timeout to chat with the willowy high school girl distributing bottles of water.

Brendan shook his head. "Doesn't he realize she's wearing a Raiders jersey?"

"I don't think he cares," Lily murmured. "There's still plenty of time for the Conquerors to make a comeback, right?"

"A comeback would imply they'd gained some ground to begin with," Brendan said drily.

Lily nibbled on her bottom lip as the players returned to the field and took their positions. "It's not their fault. Josiah doesn't seem to be giving the team any pointers."

"That's because they aren't playing Guitar Hero."

Lily couldn't prevent a smile. To make up for it, she swatted his arm. "Be nice," she admonished. "Everyone has different gifts."

Brendan aimed a pointed glance at the pom-poms. "So I noticed."

"I thought you were on the phone." Lily felt a blush sweep through her cheeks and go all the way to her toes. "The team was getting discouraged. Someone had to do something."

"You were a cheerleader, weren't you?"

"No." Lily didn't add that she'd always wanted to be. Shelby, the captain of their high school squad, had begged her to attend tryouts at the start of every school year. Lily didn't, only because she knew her father wouldn't like her indulging in what he considered frivolous pursuits. The only extracurricular activities that met with his approval were the ones guaranteed to look good on her college résumé. Business Club. Young Entrepreneurs.

"Uh-huh." Brendan looked skeptical. "It's nothing to be embarrassed about."

"I'm not…" Lily paused as a thought suddenly

occurred to her. "What makes you think I was a cheerleader?"

"Are you kidding?" Brendan laughed. "Acute case of perkiness—"

"Hey!"

"Overdeveloped sense of enthusiasm."

Lily folded her arms. "You make me sound like a disease."

Brendan ignored her as he continued to tick things off an invisible list. "Bright eyes."

Lily couldn't resist the temptation to roll them. "What does that have to do with anything?"

"Spontaneous."

"Hold it right there, buddy." Lily leaned in. "Did you just call me *spontaneous?*"

Brendan matched her another quarter inch until their noses were almost touching. "With a capital *S*."

Lily blinked. Spontaneous? The girl who'd spent the majority of her life governed by other people's expectations? The girl whose calendar, up until a few short weeks ago, had been dictated by the projects stacked up on her desk?

Lily had asked God to change her and maybe, just maybe, this was the proof. Brendan didn't realize the gift he'd just given her. Lily had tried so hard to make herself into the person she thought her father wanted her to be, she'd somehow lost herself along the way.

"You're smiling."

"Am I?" Lily touched her finger to her lips and found it was true.

Brendan's eyes narrowed. "I forgot one."

"What?" Lily tilted her chin up and looked him straight in the eye. Nothing Brendan the Brusque said now could extinguish the joy bubbling up inside of her. In fact, Lily was tempted to hug the man. But that would be—she tamped down a giggle—*spontaneous*.

Brendan's gaze dropped to her lips and lingered there. The flame in the blue eyes darkened to cobalt.

"Beautiful smile."

It was the truth, but Brendan couldn't believe he'd actually said the words out loud. Less than five minutes ago, he'd had to remind himself to keep his head in the game.

Lily's smile slipped a notch. For some reason, the compliment didn't garner the same reaction it had when Brendan had called her spontaneous.

Why not?

Brendan wanted to ask, but the words stuck in his throat. No doubt they'd gotten tangled up in the breath that emptied from his lungs when their eyes met.

Something passed between them....

"Do mind if we sit with you?"

A shadow, that's what it was. Cast by Seth and Rebecca Tamblin. The pastor and his wife stood less than a foot away, smiling down at them.

Brendan practically came out of the chair, putting some space between him and Lily—*how had they ended up so close together, anyway?*—and felt himself flush like a guilty teenager when he saw the open amusement on Seth's face.

That's what happened when a man wasn't paying attention. An ambush. Rebecca was holding hands with their three-year-old daughter, a miniature replica of her mother, while Seth cradled a chubby-cheeked baby in his arms. Behind them, staring at Lily, stood a small contingent of parents dressed in blue-and-white.

"Of course." Lily was already scooting her chair to make room. Away from his, Brendan couldn't help but notice.

Seth made the necessary introductions as the parents, most former classmates of Brendan's, began to set up camp. The chairs unfolding in a circle around him made escape impossible.

He closed his eyes.

An ambush *and* an invasion.

Chapter Nine

Brendan tugged the brim of his ball cap down an inch to shield his eyes from the sun—and the curious looks cast in his direction.

"We had to wait until the baby woke up from his nap before we could come down to the field to watch the game." The owners of the local hardware store—and former classmates of Brendan—parked a stroller roughly the size of a Volkswagen Beetle in a patch of shade next to his chair.

"That's our daughter, Josie." The woman pointed to a little girl sitting cross-legged in the grass, braiding dandelions into a chain. "This is the first time she's ever played soccer."

"Really?" Brendan tried his best to keep a straight face.

Rebecca Tamblin gathered the sweet-faced toddler onto her lap and smiled at Lily. "Seth mentioned you might be interested in attending our women's book group. We'll be meeting again on Friday morning in the fireplace room at the church."

Brendan, who'd expected Lily to tell the pastor's wife she wouldn't be in Castle Falls long enough to *read* a book, almost fell out of his chair when she nodded.

"I'd love to."

"Some of the men meet at the same time." Seth turned to Brendan. "We're reading through the gospel of Luke this summer."

"There's a combined fellowship time afterward." His wife made no secret of the fact she'd been eavesdropping. "Nothing formal...just coffee and doughnuts and a chance to get to know each other better."

Which was exactly the reason Brendan had never attended in the past and didn't plan to attend in the future.

"I'll be working Friday morning." He glanced at Lily to see if she'd taken the hint.

No, she was cooing at the Tamblins' rosy-cheeked baby, who had somehow ended up in her arms.

"If you change your mind, let Lily know." Rebecca flashed a bright smile. "You two can always carpool."

Brendan had heard rumors the pastor's wife was a notorious matchmaker. He wouldn't be surprised to discover that she and Sunni were in cahoots.

A shout from the referee pulled everyone's attention back to the field as the ball shot through the Raider's front line. It skipped across the grass, straight toward one of the Conqueror boys.

Brendan leaped to his feet. "Tackle!"

The player in blue-and-white looked startled and then launched himself at his opposing teammate instead of the ball.

The two boys rolled over the white line spray-painted in the grass.

Seriously?

Brendan clapped a hand over his eyes and groaned. "Not *that* kind of tackle."

Half a dozen pairs of eyes swung around to stare at him. So did Lily.

"You play soccer, Kane?" one of the dads asked.

"I'm…" Brendan wasn't sure why he hesitated. "Familiar with the game."

If a person counted the street hockey he'd played in a garbage-strewn alley of the housing project where he'd spent the first fifteen years of his life.

"This is the first year the kids from church formed a team. What are they doing wrong?" Josie's mother wanted to know.

Everything, Brendan was tempted to say. Until he received the silent message in Lily's eyes and obediently recited it out loud. "Nothing a few extra practices won't fix." *Or a coach who actually knows how to play the game.*

Lily's lips twitched, a sure sign she'd read his mind. Brendan wasn't sure what to do with that. Run away? Retreat?

Reach for her again?

Cassie, the Conquerors goalie, ducked to avoid the ball as it hurtled into the net. A cheer went up from the parents from the opposing team.

The referee blew the whistle, and the Conquerors slunk back to the bench. Josiah had his cell phone pressed against his ear, hands slicing the air like a ninja, wearing a path in the grass as he paced back and forth.

"Halftime," Seth announced.

Brendan tried to hide his relief. He angled closer to Lily but not so close—this time—that he jeopardized his focus. "You don't mind if we leave, do you?" He pitched his voice a few notches lower than the lively chatter going on around them.

Lily matched his whisper. "Already?"

"I have a few things to finish up this evening." Like finding a new buyer for six canoes and preparing for a phone conference with Bridges.

"If we leave now, the team will think it's because we've given up on them," she protested.

And the team would be right, Brendan thought. He shoved his fingers through his hair. "It's too late to turn things around..."

Too late, he saw a warning flash in Lily's violet eyes as her gaze locked on something—or someone—right behind him.

Dread pooled in Brendan's stomach as he pivoted around and came face-to-sad-face with Cassie Leighton. The little girl began to fold in on herself like a balloon with a slow leak as her gaze shifted from him—Brendan, the fair-weather fan—to Lily, the head cheerleader.

"It's over," the little girl mumbled.

"No, it's not." Lily looked so confident, even Brendan was tempted to believe her. "There's still another half left in the game."

"I know we have more time." Tears swam in Cassie's brown eyes. "But we don't have a coach. He left."

"Left?" Lily echoed the word.

Brendan scanned the field and outlying area, but there was no sign of Josiah. "The garage band must have taken priority."

"We can't play without a coach," Cassie moaned. "We don't know what to do!"

Seth, who'd picked up the thread of conversation, looked concerned. "What happens now?"

A murmur of alarm swept through the Conqueror parents and they pressed in closer to find out what was happening.

"Do we have to forfeit?" Rebecca asked.

Considering the score was six to zero, Brendan thought that wasn't a bad idea. Until Lily started shaking her head.

"The kids will be crushed if they have to quit in the middle of the game," she said. "Someone will have to take Josiah's place."

Back up the truck. Why was Lily looked at him? Why was *everyone* looking at him?

No. No. *"No."* Now Brendan was the one shaking his head.

"You said you played soccer. That means you know the rules, right?" one of the dads pressed.

"I—" Brendan glanced around, searching for an escape route and ran smack-dab into Rebecca Tamblin's megawatt smile.

"You certainly can't be any worse than..." The pastor's wife caught herself. "Someone with no experience at all. None of us have played. It was just basketball, baseball and football when we were growing up."

Unfortunately, Brendan thought, she had a point.

"Are you going to be our coach, Mr. Kane?" Another one of the players had somehow crashed the huddle and overheard their conversation.

"Please be our coach!" Chloe Leighton wiggled in beside her twin sister.

Great. Now he was being tag-teamed by two pint-size manipulators. Over their heads, Brendan's gaze collided with Lily's, and she had the audacity to wink at him.

"It will be—"

"Fun. I know," Brendan interrupted. "What's tomorrow's word of the day?"

Lily grinned.

"I'll let you know."

"Okay, how did you accomplish the impossible?" The slender woman with chestnut hair behind the counter at The Happy Cow whispered the question as she handed Lily a tall fluted glass layered with ice-cream and hot fudge.

"Our amazing comeback?" Lily knew she couldn't take the credit. Brendan had saved the day. Not only had he stepped in and taken Josiah's place as substitute coach, he'd been…well…amazing. Patient. Attentive. Encouraging to the players who'd looked to him for direction during the second half of the game.

"No." The woman shook her head. "Convincing Brendan Kane to darken the door of my ice cream shop. All these years, I assumed the guy was lactose intolerant."

Come to think of it, Lily was a little surprised Brendan hadn't used that as an excuse when she'd pulled him aside after the game and suggested they celebrate.

"I hate to break this to you, Lily, but we *lost,*" Brendan had murmured.

"We almost won," she corrected. "And The Happy Cow just rose to the top of my list."

Lily could tell from Brendan's expression he remembered the conversation with his brothers on the way to church that morning.

"You want ice cream? Now?" The frown had made its regularly scheduled appearance, but Lily wasn't intimidated. Not by the man who'd whipped off his blue-and-white ball cap and sent it soaring into the air with a loud whoop when Josie, still wearing her dandelion crown, got a breakaway and scored the first goal for the Conquerors.

"Let's get one thing straight," Lily informed him solemnly. "I always want ice cream, and it's Triple-Scoop Tuesday. But it would be good for the team. A bonding experience."

"If I say no, are you going to call in the Leighton twins in as reinforcements?"

"Absolutely."

"Fine." Brendan's eyes had crinkled at the corners, a dead giveaway that he wasn't as opposed to the plan as he wanted her to believe.

Lily could have released a victory whoop of her own when Brendan motioned the team back to the bench. The minute after he extended the invitation, the players rushed over to their families. The parents' smiles were all the evidence Lily needed to prove they weren't quite ready for the afternoon to end.

If Lily were totally honest, she hadn't wanted it to end, either. She liked the relaxed Brendan. The smiling Brendan. The sun-kissed, adorably rumpled Brendan.

She liked him…a lot.

Lily's stomach turned a slow cartwheel.

Liking Brendan was *not* part of the mission to get him to see there was a world beyond the four walls of his office.

"Um…Lily?" The woman behind the counter cleared her throat. "You're going to have to drink your hot fudge sundae through a straw if you don't come back to earth."

Lily snapped to attention and said the first words that popped into her head. "You know my name?"

"Lily Michaels. Designer painter. Champion of stray basset hounds. Head cheerleader for the Conquerors."

"Wow. That's…" Lily drew a blank. She really didn't know what it was.

"Incredible? Scary? Incredibly scary?" The woman laughed.

Lily bobbed her head. "All of the above."

"I'm Anna Leighton." The woman reached across the counter to shake Lily's hand. "My daughters are on the Conquerors soccer team."

"Cassie and Chloe." Lily was surprised she hadn't noticed the resemblance right away. Anna's chestnut hair was several shades darker than her adorable copper-top twins, but all three Leightons had thick-lashed, golden-brown eyes the color of maple syrup.

"I have to work longer in the evenings during the summer, so I didn't get to see the game. The good thing about a small town, you don't have to wait for the six o'clock news to find out what's happening."

"The girls did great out there," Lily told her. "On the field and off."

"Thank you." Anna fairly glowed with maternal pride. "I hope I can make it to some of the games, but this is my busiest time of year."

"I can see why." Lily picked out the maraschino

cherry crowning the top of the sundae and popped it into her mouth, savoring the burst of sweetness. "This frozen custard tastes amazing."

"Secret family recipe." Anna winked. "Passed down from my grandmother, to my mother and then to me. Along with the ancient building and the bills that inevitably go along with maintaining it, of course."

Affection rather than complaint flowed through the words. Anna's upbeat attitude reminded Lily of Shelby, and she felt an instant kinship with the woman.

"You'll have to start your own chain." Lily plunked down on one of the vinyl-covered stools that lined the counter. "A whole herd of Happy Cows."

"Right now, I'd settle for customers that crave an ice cream cone in January." Anna reached into the case and dished up another scoop of ice cream. "I've been thinking about adding a grill."

"Because burgers and fries aren't seasonal?" Lily guessed.

"Exactly." Anna gestured to the last boy in line and handed him a cone with a double scoop of chocolate ice cream. "Here you go."

His eyes went wide. "I only have a dollar."

"It's taken care of, remember?" Lily whispered.

"Oh, yeah." He beamed up at her. "Thanks!"

"Don't thank me," Lily whispered. "Thank Mr. Kane."

"Okay!" Lifting the cone in the air like a trophy,

the boy darted back to a crowded table near the window. The table where Brendan sat, hemmed in on every side by children in blue-and-white jerseys.

Should she rescue him?

Lily pondered the question for a moment and gave in to a smile. No. Way.

"Brendan is taking care of the bill?" The flicker of astonishment Lily saw in Anna's eyes was becoming all too familiar.

"He substituted for the substitute coach the second half of the game." Lily wasn't sure why she felt the need to defend him.

"Is something wrong?"

"Wrong?" Anna tipped her head. "No. It's just that Brendan Kane doesn't have a reputation for being the most…social…guy in Castle Falls."

Lily propped her elbows on the counter and leaned forward.

"What does he have a reputation for?"

Chapter Ten

Lily knew she was fishing for information, but that didn't prevent the question from tumbling out.

"He…he's a hard worker," Anna said after a moment.

It was the slight hesitation that prompted Lily to ask another.

"Did you and Brendan go to school together?"

She was a stranger to the community, and yet it hadn't escaped her notice that Brendan was the one who'd been the recipient of the openly curious looks cast in their direction all day.

"Brendan was two years ahead of me." Anna grabbed a dishrag and began to wipe down the counter. "His brother and I were in the same grade."

"Which one?" Liam and Aiden appeared to be so close in age, Lily doubted there was more than two years separating them.

"Liam." Anna seemed to stumble over the name and twin spots of color appeared in her cheeks.

Interesting reaction.

Although Lily doubted many women would have a built-in immunity to Liam Kane's dark good looks and glacier-blue eyes.

"You two dated?"

"No!" Anna ducked her head and proceeded to attack an invisible stain near the sink. "He and I sat across from each other in study hall, that's all."

Considering the young woman's blush had deepened to crimson, Lily wondered if that were completely true.

"In my high school, Brendan Kane and his brothers would have been on the top rung of the popularity ladder," she ventured.

"Maybe your high school." A shadow passed through Anna's light brown eyes.

"But not here?" Lily felt a pinch of guilt for being so pushy, but she knew she hadn't imagined the invisible wall between Brendan and the parents who'd gathered around them at the soccer game. Or the tension between Brendan and Seth Tamblin when the pastor had invited him to attend the men's study group at church. Lily had sensed it wasn't the first time the pastor had extended an invitation—and received a polite refusal in return.

"Not here," Anna echoed, her voice soft with regret. "The Brothers Grimm—that's what everyone called them. It wasn't very nice, but you know how kids can be. Under the circumstances, it couldn't have been easy for Li—for *them*. Moving from Detroit to a town the size of Castle Falls."

What circumstances?

Another tweak to her conscience had Lily biting her lip to keep from voicing the thought aloud. She didn't want Anna to think she was indulging in idle gossip, but there had to be a story here. One that might explain Brendan's reaction to her innocent comment about what it must have been like growing up in Castle Falls. Lily could still see the flash of pain in his eyes before he'd shut down the conversation.

"I'm sure it was an adjustment," Lily said carefully.

"That's an understatement." Anna sighed. "But you know how great Sunni is. She tried to get the boys involved in extracurricular activities at school, but they kept to themselves. Especially after…" Anna's slim shoulders lifted and fell, as if she expected Lily to fill in the blank.

The trouble was, at the moment, Lily had more questions than answers. But the way Anna was practically wearing a hole through the glossy varnish on the countertop with the dishrag warned Lily it was time to change the subject.

"Actually, I haven't met Sonia yet," Lily admitted. "She left on her vacation cruise the day I got here. We communicated by email and phone a few times, though. She seems like a great person."

"Everyone loves Sunni Mason." Anna's warm

smile returned. "Our church youth group used to go to their place once a summer and take a day-long canoe trip down the river.

"Sunni and her husband, Rich, were our guides and they were great. They waved the rental fees on the canoes and guide service and provided a picnic lunch at the base of falls."

Lily frowned. "You mean they used to actually take people out on the river?"

"All summer and into the fall color season. It was a big part of their business. Not only tourists, but people in town who had family visiting scheduled outings. Fishing trips. Overnight campouts."

"When did they stop?"

"The summer after Rich died, the sign on the road came down. They kept building canoes but that was it. No more trips down the river. No more picnics at the falls." Anna poured a glass of ice water and set it down on the counter in front of Lily. "There are always rumors that fly around but no one really knows why they shut that part of the business down."

Lily's gaze shifted to the table by the window.

The people in Castle Falls might not know why things had changed at Castle Falls Outfitters, but she had a strong suspicion that Brendan did.

On any other day, the four red canoes lined up on the grass outside the shop would have been a source of pride for Brendan. Proof that Castle Falls Outfitters was doing well. At this particular moment in time, they were simply a reminder of just how precarious owning a small business could be. And how much he was dreading the conversation he was about to have with his brothers.

Brendan pushed open the back door and walked into the shop. A George Strait tune filtered through the dusty speakers, accompanied by the low hum of the ceiling fan. He picked his way through the tools scattered on the floor around the workbench, but there was no sign of his brothers anywhere. When he and Lily had returned from town, Brendan had heard Liam and Aiden bantering back and forth, but he'd decided to wait to break the news about the canceled order.

The prototype for one of Liam's latest designs was elevated on a wooden frame. Brendan had made a point to mention his middle brother's vision to improve the line during one of his conversations with Garrett Bridges, and the CEO had promised to take a look at Liam's designs after they signed the contract.

After.

Brendan had grabbed the word and held on. Right now, it was the only hope he had that Castle Falls Outfitters and Extreme Adventures were close to forming a lasting partnership.

Brendan poked his head in the back room, but there was no one there.

He retraced his steps back to the house, where the tantalizing aroma of fresh baked bread and garlic wafted through the screens. He should have checked the kitchen first.

Sure enough, his brothers were dismantling a mountain of golden-brown breadsticks glistening with melted butter, piled high on a platter in the center of the kitchen table.

Brendan shook his head. "You two do have a kitchen in your apartment, you know."

Liam shrugged. "Ours isn't the same."

"He means it doesn't have food," Aiden interjected. "At least, not like this."

"Does Lily know you scavengers are here?"

"She's the one who invited us over. She said, and I quote, 'It's a breadstick kind of day.'"

A wry smile curved the corner of Brendan's lips. He figured it must have been an ice-cream kind of day, too. Lily had been right about celebrating, though. The treat afterward had soothed any leftover sting from the game and the players had chattered about their next one as if they were actually looking forward to it.

The Lily effect, Brendan had secretly dubbed it. Those violet eyes and winsome smile called to a person like the river. Gentle. Soothing. Until all of a sudden, you realized you were in way over your head....

"I like breadstick kind of days." Aiden was reaching for another one. "Can you grab the iced tea out of the fridge, Bren? Lily said she made a fresh pitcher."

"No problem."

The sarcasm was lost on his brothers, but Brendan didn't mind delaying the inevitable a few more seconds. He opened the fridge—filled with enough fresh produce to stock a farmer's market stand—and grabbed the container of iced tea from the shelf.

"What's up, bro?" Liam had a bead on him. Brendan could only guess what Mr. Intuitive had seen on his face.

The fact Brendan had rehearsed the words on his way to the house didn't mean they were going to be easy to say. He leaned a hip against the butcher block island and took the plunge. "We lost the Jenkins order."

Aiden started choking on a breadstick, and Liam poured a glass of tea and pushed it across the table.

"That's six canoes," he said quietly.

"I'm aware." Brendan released a slow breath. "Four are ready to go, right? An email came in this morning from someone interested in purchasing two canoes."

"Recreational?"

"Solo. But you never know, they might appreciate a little more space."

His brothers' expressions didn't change. They'd already done the math and both of them knew that interest didn't always guarantee a sale.

"We'll move them," Brendan said, praying it was true. "Don't worry. I've got this."

"That's what he always says." Aiden rolled his eyes at Liam, but his shoulders relaxed. The air in the room suddenly felt lighter, as if Brendan's words had punctured a hole in the tension.

How many times had he made that same promise to his siblings over the years and witnessed the same response?

"No Christmas bonus this year." Liam nudged Aiden, who grinned.

"Or Thanksgiving turkey."

Their unwavering trust had always been humbling. And terrifying.

Memories began to bleed into Brendan's conscience and he was powerless to stem the flow.

Herding Liam and Aiden into the safety of his bedroom closet when their mother's current boyfriend staggered into the house after bar close, broke and belligerent and looking for a fight. Sorting through piles of blue jeans and T-shirts at the thrift store when Liam and Aiden needed clothes for school. Slipping in through the back door of a church-run shelter in their neighborhood to grab boxes of macaroni and cheese from the supply closet because his pride prevented him from standing in line.

The supply closet where he'd met Rich Mason for the very first time.

In his mind's eye, Brendan could still see a bear of a man with a russet beard filling the doorway, blocking his escape. Indecision had glued Brendan's feet to the floor. If he dropped the armload of canned food, Liam and Aiden wouldn't have anything to eat.

If he didn't, they wouldn't have a brother around to make *sure* they ate.

"Looks like a heavy load," the man had rumbled. *"Let me help you with that."*

Brendan had no choice but to drop everything on the scarred linoleum floor and run.

He'd never expected the guy to follow him. Or that he would show up at Brendan's door the next day with the very food he had attempted to steal. That encounter had changed Brendan's life.

It had changed Rich Mason's, too.

Regret no longer sent a chill running through Brendan. It had settled deep, leaving a permanent ache all the way down to the marrow.

"Sit down for a minute." The heels of Liam's chair scraped the floor. He stretched out his legs.

"I don't have a minute." And Brendan didn't trust the gleam of amusement in Liam's eyes. "I still have a few more hours of work waiting for me."

"I wonder why." Aiden grinned.

Brendan ignored the innuendo. If he told his brothers that Lily had coerced him into treating the entire soccer team to ice cream at The Happy Cow, he'd never hear the end of it.

Brendan took a step toward the refrigerator and almost stepped on a furry brown tail. The dog was camped under the table, waiting for a crumb to fall.

"What are you doing here?" Brendan realized he'd directed the question at Missy when Aiden burst out laughing. He scowled at his youngest brother. "What is she doing here?"

"Lily asked if we'd keep an eye on her for a little while."

Aiden tore into another breadstick. "At least take one of these with you."

"Why?"

"Because they're delicious…and they'll be gone in about sixty seconds if you don't."

Brendan counted to ten—slowly—before he rephrased the question. "Why did Lily ask you to keep an eye on Missy?"

"She said she had something to do." Aiden rocked back on his chair. "Maybe an errand to run in town."

"We were already there." Brendan glanced out the window and saw Lily's car parked in front of the garage.

Amusement lit Liam's eyes. "We know."

This was one conversation Brendan didn't intend to have with his brothers.

"Lily said she wouldn't be gone more than an hour or so."

Liam took pity on Missy and fed her a piece of breadstick. "She's a grown woman, Bren. I'm sure she's fine."

Brendan didn't like the look his brothers exchanged. Like they knew something he didn't. "What?"

"Nothing."

"Right." When Aiden got that look in his eye, Brendan knew it was always something.

Liam, the traitor, was nodding in agreement. "She looks like a woman who can handle herself."

That's what Brendan was afraid of.

But *what* was she going to handle?

An image of Lily skipping across a log over the churning water flashed in his mind.

Tension pooled in Brendan's gut even as his mind rejected the thought.

She wouldn't…

I have one more thing to do this evening, she'd said when they had returned from town.

The invisible list she pulled out on a moment's notice.

"Isn't she supposed to be painting?" Brendan glared at the sheep on the wall.

"It's seven o'clock at night, Bren. She doesn't need your permission to have a little fun while she's here."

Fun.

There was only one thing Brendan could think of that fit the criteria.

The cave.

Brendan made it to the falls in record time and looked for signs that Lily had gotten there ahead of him.

God, please, if she's in there, keep her safe.

The prayer formed in his heart and took wing as Brendan kicked off his shoes and began the precarious climb up the rock wall that bracketed the falls.

At the top, the memory of the last time he had entered the tunnel sent a wave of dizziness spiraling through him.

But if Lily was inside…

Brendan closed his eyes, ducked his head, and plunged through the heavy curtain of water.

Lily heard a…sound.

Not quite a snap. Not quite a thump. Something in between.

The cold water dripping down the back of Lily's neck was no longer the most disturbing thing in the tunnel. It suddenly occurred to her that the only thing worse than being alone in a pitch-black, creepy tunnel was sharing the space with whatever *thing* might consider the pitch-black, creepy tunnel home.

She swallowed down the panic crawling up the back of her throat.

How had she gotten herself into this predicament, anyway?

One minute Lily had been sliding the last pan of homemade breadsticks out of the oven, an activity she'd hoped would keep her thoughts from drifting to a certain blue-eyed substitute soccer coach, when Liam and Aiden had sauntered into the kitchen.

The two men had practically swooned when Lily set the plate down in the middle of the table and told them to help themselves.

Aiden had claimed one of the wooden chairs at the table and settled in. "How was the picnic? We figured you'd be back— *Ouch*." The table jerked and he speared Liam with a look. "A long time ago."

Lily thought of Brendan's reaction to the burned hot dogs and smiled. "There was a game afterward, so we stayed to watch."

Liam's eyebrows popped. "Brendan stayed for a soccer game?"

"He was the guest of honor." Lily poured warm marinara sauce in a bowl and handed it to Aiden. "He had to."

Brendan's brothers exchanged what Lily was starting to silently refer to as The Look.

"It was a good thing he stayed, because he ended up filling in for the coach," Lily continued. "We didn't win, but the score was so close, we took the team out for ice cream to celebrate."

If the pyramid of breadsticks in the center of the table had suddenly burst into flames, Lily doubted she would have witnessed such a strong reaction.

"Because he had to?" Liam queried.

"Right." Lily had ignored the laughter dancing in his eyes.

"I can't remember the last time Brendan took an entire evening off," Aiden mused.

"I can't remember the last time he took time off, period," Liam added. "We'll have to tag along next time and take notes. See how you do it."

"I didn't *do* anything," Lily had protested.

She also doubted there was going to *be* a next time. When they'd left The Happy Cow, Lily had

had a difficult time keeping up with Brendan. He'd practically jogged to the truck in his haste to get back to the office.

Or get away from her. A distinct—but rather depressing, Lily couldn't deny it—possibility, as well.

"You don't know our brother," Aiden said slowly. "Brendan doesn't do anything he doesn't want to do. Not soccer. Not ice cream."

It crossed Lily's mind that maybe it was his family who didn't know him as well as they thought they did.

"He seemed to enjoy himself."

"Oh, I'm sure he did."

Aiden's comment reminded Lily of the soccer game. Which in turn reminded her of the way Brendan had teased her. Smiled at her. The look in his eyes when his gaze had dropped to her lips.

Had he thought about kissing her?

She fanned herself with the potholder.

"Getting warm in here, isn't it?" Liam's innocent comment was a counterbalance to the gleam in his eyes.

"Yes. I think… Can you watch Missy for a little while?"

Lily had done the only thing she could do given the circumstances. She'd decided to retreat to a place where she could untangle her muddled thoughts.

She'd promised Shelby she would call later that evening to give her an update. Knowing her friend's penchant for reading between the lines, Lily decided she better have something to talk about that would pique Shelby's interest more than the hours she'd spent with Brendan.

The only thing that came to mind was the cave Liam and Aiden had told her about. Peaceful. Quiet. A place to be alone with her muddled thoughts.

Except that she wasn't alone.

Lily heard another thump. Definitely a thump this time.

Her heart responded in kind.

Lord, I'm not alone, am I? You're right here and You'll protect me from...whatever is out there.

Because whatever was out there was getting closer.

Chapter Eleven

Lily blamed Brendan for her current predicament.

After all, he was the one who'd called her spontaneous. The description had obviously gone to her head. The very word tasted sweet on Lily's tongue. It was all about embracing possibilities and trying something new. Stepping off the path of the familiar.

Which would have been easier if Lily hadn't dropped her flashlight.

It was a little difficult to admit that all her new-found courage had fled the moment some tiny creature had skittered over her feet in the darkness. She'd jumped a foot in the air and bumped her head against the ceiling. The flashlight dropped out of her hand and rolled away, flashing a brief SOS before it conked out and left Lily stranded in indecision. Admit defeat and make her way back to the entrance or keep moving forward into the unknown?

Half an hour later, she was still trying to choose between the two.

At least no was around to witness her predicament...

"Lily?"

A familiar voice rumbled through the darkness.

Lily sagged against the rock wall and pressed one hand against her heart in an attempt to hold it in place.

"I'm...here," she croaked.

"Okay." A short but significant pause followed. And then, "Are you coming out?"

Lily knew she'd been in the dark too long when she found the low rasp of Brendan's voice, embedded with shards of frustration, more soothing than disturbing.

Brendan doesn't do anything he doesn't want to do, Aiden had said. Well, here was proof to the contrary. Once again, he'd been forced to track her down.

"Eventually." Lily had to be honest.

"Are you hurt?"

She debated for a moment whether to count the self-inflicted, rapidly swelling lump on the top of her head. "N-no." Unfortunately, a slight hitch separated the one syllable word into two, making Lily's reply sound less than convincing. Maybe Brendan wouldn't pick up on it....

"I'll be right there."

He'd picked up on it.

Relief and trepidation twisted together and formed a knot in her stomach.

"Are we playing hide-and-seek?" Brendan's voice

filtered through the darkness. "Say something so I can find you."

A word popped into Lily's head and she said it out loud.

"Marco."

Silence. She couldn't hear shuffling or splashing or even muttering.

"Polo."

Lily swallowed hard as Brendan's breath fanned out against her cheek. The scent of fresh pine filled the space around her. The real McCoy, not the kind that was mass-produced and sold by the bottle in upscale department stores.

"Hi," Lily managed to gasp.

A pinpoint of light illuminated Brendan's chiseled features. The concern she saw reflected in his eyes appeared to be genuine.

"Are you sure you're not hurt?" A large, warm hand skated down her arm, leaving a trail of goose bumps in its wake.

"I'm—" It suddenly hurt to breathe, did that count? "—fine."

"Then why aren't you moving?"

"Your brothers forgot to tell me the tunnel narrowed in the center," Lily managed.

Brendan's eyebrow shot up. "You're blaming this on my brothers?"

"No." Well. Maybe a little.

When Liam and Aiden had described the passageway leading to the cave, they'd somehow forgotten to mention a key piece of information. The tunnel was shaped like an hourglass. In her defense, Lily had been doing *fine* until she'd tried to squeeze through the spot where it narrowed. That's when the unknown critter had tap-danced over her feet and she'd dropped the flashlight.

"It's been years since Liam and Aiden were here," Brendan ground out. "They probably didn't remember."

Lily lifted her chin. "I'm only saying that if I'd known the layout of the tunnel, I would have been more prepared."

"You. Prepared." Brendan's eyes narrowed. "You are the most..." He seemed to be struggling to find the right word.

"Spontaneous," Lily said helpfully.

"Impulsive." Brendan leaned forward and practically growled the word in her ear.

"That's not true," she shot back. "I was planning this all afternoon."

The moment the words tumbled out, Lily braced herself for the fallout. Worst-case scenario, the man would have her arrested for trespassing and tossed off the property. Best-case scenario? At the moment, she couldn't think of one.

The last thing she expected to see was the smile that pulled at the corners of his lips.

"Exasperating." Brendan raked his hand through his hair. "I can't believe you decided to explore the cave on your own."

"I didn't," Lily muttered.

"Didn't what?"

"Explore the cave."

"Why not?"

"Because I got…stuck."

"Stuck?" Panic turned up the heat in Brendan's eyes. "How?"

He didn't wait for an answer. His hands skimmed over her shoulders and down her arms, searching for the slightest abnormality, like a coach would do for an injured player. His touch was strong but gentle and when his fingers traced the curve of her hip, both her knees turned to liquid.

"I'm not stuck like *that,*" she said breathlessly.

Brendan's head snapped up. "What do you mean? How many kinds of 'stuck' are there?"

Way too many. "You wouldn't understand."

"Try me."

"I couldn't decide what to do," Lily confessed. "I lost my flashlight somewhere, and I knew once I found it, I'd have to decide to whether to go back or keep moving forward. So I…stopped."

"So you were stuck in a…quandary?"

Lily heaved a sigh. "Exactly."

Brendan stared down at her as if she was some exotic, previously undiscovered creature he had stumbled upon, one that scientists hadn't had a chance to label.

Lilium spontaneousus.

Lily pressed her fingers against her lips to prevent a gurgle of laughter from escaping.

Brendan simply shook his head. The beam of light on his cell phone shifted away from her face and zigzagged over the floor of the tunnel.

"It's right over here." He stooped down to retrieve it. The light chased the shadows into the corners of the tunnel as Brendan handed it back to her. "Here you go. Now, let's get out of here."

Lily balked. "But—"

"But. What?"

"It's just that I'm so…close."

"You want to keep going?"

Brendan battled an overwhelming urge to toss Lily over his shoulder and carry her back to the entrance of the tunnel. When he'd called her name and heard the faint response, the slight wobble in her voice, images tumbled through his mind like dominoes. Rock walls crumbling. Lily caught in the debris.

Brendan had been forced to fold almost in half as he entered the tunnel. It was a lot smaller than he remembered. He'd inched forward, wading through ice-cold water that sloshed around his ankles. He hadn't remembered that, either. He braced himself for the worst as he made his way toward Lily, only to find her "stuck in a quandary."

"Y-yes." Lily answered his question. The wobble had returned but the determined set of her chin told Brendan she'd made up her mind.

He aimed the light at the place where the tunnel narrowed to a span of about two feet. A curtain of darkness hung beyond the reach of the light, so thick he couldn't see what lay ahead.

"You don't have to go with me, you know. Now that I have the flashlight, I'll be fine." Lily mustered a brave smile.

Brendan sighed. "Let's go."

Lily tipped her head. "Forward?"

Against his better judgment. "Forward."

She bent down to retrieve a brightly colored backpack, one Brendan hadn't noticed until now, and slid her arms through the straps.

"Ready!"

Brendan wished he could say the same. He turned sideways in order to squeeze through the narrow opening. Lily followed without hesitation, radiating the same level of trust Brendan's brothers had always shown in him.

The thought had him breaking out in a cold sweat.

Lily hopped over a pile of crumbled rock and jostled for position in the narrow passageway. The backpack shifted and threw Lily off balance. They stumbled, feet tangling together like a couple taking their first ballroom dance lesson. Brendan automatically reached out to steady Lily and his hand molded to the curve of her hip at the same time she grabbed hold of his arm. They began to teeter.

Brendan's breath hissed between his teeth as he

set Lily firmly back on her feet. "The guy is supposed to lead."

Lily's teeth flashed white in the gloom. "I'll try to remember that."

Brendan surged forward. Whatever lay ahead wasn't nearly as dangerous as the attraction simmering between them.

No immunity to her smile. No immunity to her sense of humor.

He was in big trouble.

"Watch your head," Brendan cautioned. "The height of the ceiling drops a few inches right before the cave."

"We're almost there?"

The lilt in Lily's voice conveyed her anticipation while Brendan's steps slowed.

The tunnel widened into a spacious cavern with a dome-like ceiling. Lily stopped beside him, her eyes going wide as she took in their surroundings.

"This is incredible." She turned a slow circle, enchanted by the swirls of burgundy and amber decorating the sandstone walls. "When was the last time you were here?"

Brendan looked away from Lily's shining eyes.

"I don't remember."

No, that wasn't completely true. He didn't *want* to remember. The one and only time Brendan had taken refuge in the cave, he hadn't been trying to escape the rumors about his past, he had been trying to give his brothers the chance of a future.

The day they'd arrived in Castle Falls, Brendan was under no illusion that *his* stay was permanent. For all their exuberance and wild antics, at twelve and ten years old, Liam and Aiden still had the cute factor going for them. Brendan? A budding juvenile delinquent with a chip on his shoulder and what the social worker called "authority issues."

The only thing Brendan wanted was to make sure his brothers were settled in a decent home. His younger siblings would never have agreed to move in with the Masons if Brendan hadn't been part of the package, so he'd stuffed his tattered duffle bag into the back of the Masons' truck and watched Detroit grow smaller in the rearview mirror.

Brendan hadn't been looking for trouble, but it always seemed to find him. He ignored the suspicious looks his classmates cast his way. He didn't even mind being the pariah of Emerson High School. It would have been preferable to becoming an easy target for Les Atkins, the Eagles star quarterback. The guy liked to start fires and watch other people get burned.

All heads had swung in Brendan's direction the day Les sauntered out of the locker room and informed the coach that his watch was missing.

Brendan saw the smirk on Les's face and knew no one would believe he was innocent—especially when the watch was discovered in Brendan's backpack. The judgment handed down by the principal was a week-long suspension, but Brendan figured he wouldn't make it that long. Rich and Sunni Mason would ship him back to Detroit within twenty-four hours.

He decided to leave before the couple could kick him out, but he wanted to stick around a few days to make sure his brothers didn't suffer from his mistakes. The cave he'd discovered behind the falls would provide a temporary refuge.

Brendan had told Liam and Aiden his plan and sworn them to secrecy. When Rich showed up the next day, it had felt more like a betrayal than Atkins accusing him of a crime he didn't commit.

Brendan had expected Rich to haul him out by the collar—that's what his old man would have done before he'd taken off—but Rich had lowered himself to the cold, damp floor as if they were about to sit down for a Sunday afternoon football game.

Brendan waited for a lecture or an ultimatum. Rich hadn't delivered either one. He did, however, make Brendan an offer. An order had come in, and he needed help in the shop.

So what if he was free labor? Brendan didn't care if it meant he would have another week with his brothers.

He'd rolled out of bed the next morning and wolfed down the stack of blueberry pancakes Sunni set in front of him before heading out the door.

Brendan finally found Rich down by the river, readying one of the canoes.

"Come on."

Brendan had eyed the canoe warily. "I thought you said you had work for me to do."

"That's right." Rich tossed him a smile and a wooden paddle. "And this is where it starts."

They'd worked side by side from dawn to dusk every day that week. Rich was a patient teacher but he demanded excellence in every part of the building process. He also belted out hymns like they were at an open-air gospel sing-along while they worked, which had driven Brendan crazy.

Sunni fussed that orders were starting to pile up, but Rich didn't seem to care. Brendan decided the customer who'd ordered this particular canoe must be pretty important to receive Rich's undivided attention.

When Brendan voiced the thought aloud, Rich had looked him straight in the eye.

He is.

Brendan's throat closed as another memory crashed over him.

When the canoe was finished, Rich had given it to him.

Until then, no one had invested in Brendan's life. Deemed him worthy of their time and attention.

If only he'd had a chance to tell Rich that before he'd died.

Before Brendan had let him down.

Lily realized that Brendan hadn't moved from the entrance.

His hands were balled into fists at his sides, his

expression as shadowed as the cave. He didn't look preoccupied as much as he looked...lost. Vulnerable.

Although they were only several feet apart, Lily sensed a chasm had opened up between them. Without thinking, she reached for his hand, wanting nothing more than to free him from whatever thoughts held him captive.

"Brendan?"

His whole body stiffened and he slowly pivoted to face her.

He blinked rapidly and the shadows cleared. "Sorry. What did you say?"

"Would you like something to drink?" Lily tugged him toward the center of the cave; as if that was the reason she'd taken his hand in the first place. "I brought lemonade."

Brendan's gaze flicked to the stadium blanket she'd spread out on the floor of the cave. "And enough food to feed an army. Are you planning to move in?"

"No." Hands on her hips, Lily scanned the interior of the cave. "This place doesn't need a makeover. The walls are already beautiful."

Brendan's response was a slightly lopsided—and extremely charming—smile that gave Lily the courage to shoo him toward the snacks she'd packed. "Sit down. I don't know about you, but I'm starving."

"Really?" He hiked a brow. "Because I'm sure I heard someone complaining she ate her weight in ice cream at The Happy Cow."

Lily claimed a corner of the picnic blanket. "That was two hours ago."

"Uh-huh." Brendan dropped down across from her and Lily couldn't help but feel a sense of accomplishment.

Lily folded her hands in her lap. "Do you mind if I pray?"

"Not at all." Brendan still sounded subdued.

His whole demeanor had changed since they'd entered the cave.

Lily offered up a silent prayer of her own as she closed her eyes.

God, whatever is bothering Brendan, let him know it's okay to share the burden. Let him know You care about him.

She bowed her head. "Lord, thank You for this day. Thank You for the beauty of your creation. For every good and perfect gift You give to Your children."

Lily opened her eyes only to find Brendan glowering at her.

"You *did* get hurt."

Lily gingerly touched the lump on her head and tried not to wince. "You should see the other guy."

"You mean the rock?" Brendan shot back.

Lily grinned. "I'm sure it has a dent in it."

Brendan wasn't listening. He was too busy shaking celery sticks out of a plastic baggie and replacing them with ice cubes from her water bottle.

"Come here."

"I'm fine," Lily protested. Fine with a bit of distance and a backpack between them. Not so fine when Brendan invaded her personal space.

"You just spent half an hour in a tunnel the size of a culvert, and you didn't have a flashlight," he reminded her. "Don't be a wimp now."

"I'm not a wimp." To prove it, Lily leaned forward and tucked her chin against her chest.

"At least the skin isn't broken." Brendan pressed the makeshift ice pack against her head.

"Ouch!" Lily flinched. "That feels worse than the lump."

"Think about something else."

About the way Brendan's dark eyelashes curled slightly at the edges? Or maybe the way his blue eyes seemed to change color along with the changes in his mood?

Or the way her heart began to beat like a kettle drum whenever he touched her?

Lily had no choice but to fall back on her caregiver's childhood remedy for bruises, bumps and scrapes. She began to belt out the chorus of "Row, Row, Row Your Boat."

Now it was Brendan's turn to wince.

"What are you doing?"

"Thinking about something else."

Brendan's laughter flowed over her, as warm and inviting as the river outside his home. Caught in the undertow, Lily scrambled to keep her internal balance.

She had a feeling that keeping her feelings in line was going to be even more difficult.

Chapter Twelve

"Hold this in place for a few minutes until the swelling goes down."

Lily could deal with the swelling. At the moment, it was the erratic beat of her heart that gave her the most cause for concern.

She'd given presentations to the CEOs of major corporations and led workshops at advertising conventions all over the Midwest without the least bit of nervousness. So why did she get all tongue-tied and giddy every time Brendan looked at her? Every time he touched her?

Brendan retreated to the other side of the blanket again and Lily exhaled as her lungs resumed their work. She unpacked the rest of the contents in her backpack, all too aware that Brendan's eyes followed every movement.

Leaning back on her elbows, Lily contemplated their surroundings. "It's so peaceful here. Quiet."

"Quiet?" Brendan's voice was dry. "I hadn't noticed."

Lily wadded up her napkin and chucked it at him. "I thought Aiden was the comedian in the family."

"He is."

"I suppose being Big Brother is a full-time job."

"You've got that right." Brendan snagged a handful of carrot sticks. "By the way, you have to stop feeding them. Liam and Aiden are like a couple of bear cubs. Fuzzy and kind of cute, but once you start feeding them, they won't leave you alone."

Lily smiled. "I like your brothers."

"You don't have siblings?"

"Only child."

"So you didn't have to share your toys or your parents."

"The toys, no." Lily strove to keep her voice even. "Mom died in a car accident when I was four years old, so it was just me and my dad. He was on his way to becoming a junior partner at the law firm where he worked and didn't quite know what to do with a little girl." Lily rummaged through her picnic supplies and found a container of plastic flatware. "Try the cherry salsa. I picked it up at a farmer's stand on the way here."

Brendan didn't try the salsa. He leaned forward, staring at her with an intensity that made Lily feel as if there were a flowchart stamped on her forehead.

"That must have been difficult for him. Becoming a widower and a single parent in the blink of an eye," he said quietly.

"Nothing is difficult for Nolan Michaels." Lily

shrugged. "He arranged for a full-time caregiver and had her keep a log of what I'd accomplished that day. If it was something interesting, he would ask me about it when he got home at night."

As soon as Lily had figured that out, she made certain she'd done something that would warrant her father's undivided attention.

"So the pressure was on you."

Lily jerked a nod, a little disconcerted that Brendan had heard the words she hadn't spoken. "My father had high—"

"Expectations."

They said the word at the same time.

"Yes."

"I guess we have something in common." Brendan's rueful smile stirred the butterflies in Lily's stomach.

"We don't want to disappoint the people we care about."

Lily thought about her father's last visit. She'd tried to make him understand how important it was that she be there for Shelby, but from Nolan's perspective, she was making a mistake. Brendan's jaw tightened. His expression was identical to the one Lily had seen when he'd been on the phone at the soccer game.

Who was he afraid of disappointing?

"It's up to us to save them from the consequences of our mistakes, though," Brendan murmured.

Lily wasn't sure he'd meant to say the words out loud.

"What kind of mistakes?"

Brendan's eyes darkened and for a second, Lily was afraid she'd pushed too hard. Severed the fragile bond that connected them.

He scrubbed a hand across his jaw and looked away.

"We lost an order today."

Why had he told her that?

Brendan never discussed business with people outside the family. The truth was, unless there were unusual circumstances, Brendan didn't discuss business *with* his family.

"Does that happen a lot?"

Concern clouded Lily's eyes and Brendan shrugged.

"Once in a while a customer changes his mind, but this one happened to be a special order. Six canoes."

Lily nibbled on her lower lip. "I'm sorry."

"Liam and Aiden have four of them finished, but it will take some time to move the inventory. We're almost halfway through the summer, and sales tend to dip in the fall."

"People are thinking about back to school, not recreation," Lily murmured.

"Right." Brendan tried to hide his surprise that she had made the connection. "There are different types of canoes. We build some for fishing, some for touring. The ones they just finished for the order were designed to accommodate a family. Two seaters with room for gear."

"Not your most popular model?"

"Unfortunately, no. Most people are interested in our touring canoes because of their versatility. They handle easily on both rivers and lakes...." Brendan caught himself. "Sorry. You're probably not interested in the details."

Lily didn't seem to hear him. Her forehead puckered in a frown.

"Have you thought about placing an ad in the local newspaper?"

"No." Brendan's teeth snapped together.

A special ad? He didn't advertise in the local newspaper at all. The editor, Gavin Whitman, had made no secret of the fact he disapproved of the Masons' decision to take Brendan and his brothers into their home. To prove his point, the man had actually given Sunni a stack of newspaper articles he'd collected, highlighting all the problems with the foster-care system.

"I suppose everyone within a fifty-mile radius of Castle Falls already owns one of your canoes," Lily was saying.

"I wouldn't know. The bulk of the orders come through the website. Whoever is free delivers them, if necessary. Otherwise we'll ship directly to the customer."

"Anna Leighton mentioned that Castle Falls Outfitters used to rent out canoes."

"A long time ago." So long ago Brendan didn't think about it anymore. "It turned out to be a lot of work with very little return."

Although the Masons hadn't thought so.

When Brendan had approached Sunni about shutting that part of the business down, she hadn't completely supported the idea. She loved chatting with the people who stopped over, but after Rich died and the business was floundering, none of them had time to drop everything and take people for excursions on the river.

Brendan had been relieved when Sunni finally told him to do what he thought was best. Her unwavering trust made Brendan more determined to make Castle Falls Outfitters a success. They didn't need the help of the community—people who hadn't exactly thrown out the welcome mat to him and his brothers—to achieve that goal, either.

"Have you—"

"Yes." Brendan held up his hand. "I offer special sales throughout the season."

"I was going to ask if you'd prayed about the situation," Lily countered softly. "If there's one thing I've learned recently, it's that God doesn't set things in motion and then step back to let us figure them out. He cares about the things we care about."

Brendan remembered the way she'd prayed when they sat down. Genuine. Easy. As natural as taking her next breath. When was the last time he'd talked to God that way? If he were honest, his prayers were more like an employee checking in occasionally with the boss. A polite but concise update more than a conversation.

It had always been easier for Brendan to relay facts than deal with feelings. And right now, he was trying to avoid dealing with the feelings Lily stirred inside him.

"I'm sure God has enough to deal with. I doubt that selling canoes is high on His list of priorities," Brendan finally said.

"But *you* are."

Brendan dragged in a breath. Lily had somehow managed to read his mind again. In his head, he believed what she said was true. It wasn't as easy to embrace the idea that it was true for *him*.

"'The Lord is righteous in all his ways and loving toward all He has made. The Lord is near to all who call on Him in truth,'" Lily quoted. "It's one of the verses I memorized this week."

Call.

Brendan vaulted to his feet.

"We have to go."

Lily didn't move, so Brendan began scooping up the contents of her backpack and stuffing them into the zippered pouch.

"Why? Is something wrong?"

Everything was wrong, Brendan thought.

He'd missed Garrett Bridges's call.

* * *

Lily stepped back to admire the bare wall.

It was amazing what a girl could accomplish when she started work at five in the morning.

Three hours, one chipped fingernail and a permanent crease at the base of her spine, but she had successfully removed the last of the wallpaper sheep in the kitchen. Her cell phone began to ring, and Lily glanced at the name on the screen.

Lily wasn't sure what to deal with first. The sticky, leftover residue from the wallpaper...or the incoming call from her father.

She opted for the second, only because she wasn't convinced he wouldn't hop in the car and drive to Castle Falls if she didn't answer.

"Hi, Dad."

"I tried to call you last night," Nolan barked in her ear. "Where were you?

I'm fine, Dad. How are you?

"I was...gone for a few hours."

"And you couldn't answer the phone? It's not like you're living in a cave."

Lily nearly strangled on a breath. "The cell phone reception is spotty in places."

Like...caves.

Lily set that thought—and all the others that had come before it—firmly aside.

"When are you coming back?"

Lily dragged in a breath and silently counted to five.

"I'll be here another week. Don't you remember?"

"Maybe I would remember if you'd *told* me that was the plan," her father retorted.

Lily prayed for patience. There was no sense in reminding Nolan that she'd given him a rather detailed outline of her schedule before leaving town—he just hadn't paid attention. Conversations with her father tended to be fairly one-sided. He lectured. She listened.

"I still have several rooms left to paint." Lily strove to keep her voice even. Polite. Similar to the one she used when dealing with a particularly difficult client. "I can't walk away and leave a project unfinished."

"Isn't that what you did when you left Pinnacle?"

Lily should have known he would use the words against her.

"I have plenty of vacation time built up." Five years' worth, as a matter of fact. "This is how I'm choosing to use it. Dennis understands."

Nolan snorted. "Don't be too sure about that. I happened to see him at the country club yesterday and we golfed nine holes together."

Knowing her father, the meeting hadn't been accidental.

Nolan made no secret that he had joined the country club to improve his business relationships, not his golf game.

"How is he doing?"

"Short-handed. Dennis hinted that your timing wasn't exactly convenient."

"The timing wasn't exactly convenient for Shelby, either, Dad. She didn't plan to get sick."

"I realize that," Nolan sputtered. "But you have to keep your priorities straight."

My priorities? Or yours?

More and more, Lily was beginning to realize they weren't the same.

"Dennis will manage just fine without me for a few more days."

"You don't want your boss to 'manage just fine' without you!" Nolan growled. "Dennis told me there's a new company interested in signing with Pinnacle and the owner specifically mentioned that he wanted to work with you. This isn't the time to abandon ship."

Lily flinched. The words had become a familiar refrain over the past few weeks but that didn't lessen their sting. "I've logged more hours than anyone else in the company. Taking some time off shouldn't be viewed as abandoning ship, Dad."

"Your reputation isn't the only one at stake, you know. I'm the one—"

Who got you the job at Pinnacle.

Lily mouthed the words along with her father.

Nolan never missed an opportunity to remind Lily that he'd prevailed upon a long-standing friendship with her boss to secure an entry-level position at the company after Lily graduated from college. She had accepted the offer, not realizing it meant that her father would keep an even more watchful eye on her career.

"Dennis wouldn't be a very good friend if he held you responsible for my decisions, would he?"

"You've worked too hard for this." Lily wasn't surprised he'd avoided the question. "You don't want to do anything that might jeopardize your promotion."

"There will be other promotions."

The silence on the other end of the phone was so large Lily could have fallen into it.

"I don't know what's gotten into you lately."

"Nothing has 'gotten into me,' Dad," Lily said softly. "I…I think it was always there. I just never paid attention to it until Shelby got sick."

"I have no idea what you're talking about." Nolan sounded distant. Remote. In a way, it was worse than the silence.

Lily felt a familiar ache in her chest. No, he didn't understand. That's what bothered her the most.

"Nothing has changed, Dad. I'll be back in Traverse City next week and everything will be the same." Even as she said the words, Lily knew they weren't entirely true.

Brendan wouldn't be there.

Chapter Thirteen

Lily was afraid to analyze that thought—or why it bothered her—too closely.

Missy scrabbled over to the window, nosed the lace panel aside and began to howl.

"What is that noise?" Nolan huffed, sounding like himself again. "Are you surrounded by a pack of coyotes?"

"It's one dog, and she belongs to Sunni Mason, the woman who hired me to paint." Lily didn't mention the basset was in need of a permanent home. Or that her apartment happened to be conveniently located near the dog park. "I really have to go, Dad. Someone's here."

"Are you the official doorman now, too?"

Lily chuckled as if he were teasing. "I'll call you later."

She hung up and shot Missy a warning look when the basset hound beat her to the door, tail wagging in anticipation.

"Don't even think about it," Lily warned. Missy, the unofficial goodwill ambassador, had discovered an activity she enjoyed even more than chasing butterflies and squirrels—greeting the mail carrier and every deliveryman who stopped by the house.

Lily stepped onto the porch and shaded her eyes against the morning sun. Not a delivery truck. A sleek, charcoal-gray SUV with tinted windows was rolling up the driveway. It pulled over to the side and stopped right in front of the shop.

An attractive couple who looked to be in their late thirties emerged from the vehicle. The man wore a plaid shirt and cargo shorts paired with leather sandals, standard issue for most of the tourists passing through the area. His wife, a slender woman with a platinum, shoulder-length bob, slid on a pair of sunglasses and began to look around.

Doors popped open, and three children tumbled out of the backseat. Two preadolescent girls, all legs and arms, and a boy of about five or six who hit the ground running the moment his feet touched the driveway. The man caught him by the shirttail and tossed him over his shoulder.

The boy's giggles mingled with the wind chimes hanging from the porch.

Smiling, Lily took a step backward. If the family were lost and in need of directions, Liam would help them out.

She knew that Aiden had taken one of the canoes out shortly after breakfast. He'd stopped in the kitchen to fill up his thermos with coffee and mentioned that Brendan had left for a few hours.

Left his office. In the middle of the workday.

Lily did her best to hold her smile in place until Aiden left.

What had gone wrong?

One minute Brendan was confiding in her about the order they'd lost and the next minute, scooping everything into her backpack and urging her down the tunnel.

Lily had no idea what had caused the abrupt change in Brendan's mood, but whatever had happened, it was clear she was somehow to blame.

Brendan had barely spoken to her as they made their way back to the house. Once inside, he had veered straight down the hall and disappeared into his office.

Lily started peeling the wallpaper off the walls, hoping he would make an appearance but the snap of the door signaled he'd left the house without a word. The lights in his cabin had flickered on a few minutes later.

She was tempted to ask Aiden if everything was all right, but he'd come into the kitchen muttering something that included the words *bull-headed* and *aggravating*. Lily could only assume he'd been talking about his older brother.

For some reason, knowing she wasn't the only one feeling the fallout made Lily feel a little bit better.

"Come on, Missy. Let's go back inside."

Missy let out a low woof. The man spotted them and waved.

"Good morning!" His cheerful greeting sent a flock of birds into the air like a spray of buckshot.

Lily waved back and ambled down the steps. There was no sign of Liam, and whether Brendan approved or not, it wouldn't be polite to leave visitors standing in the driveway.

By the time Lily reached the couple's side, the man's smile had doubled in width. "Cal Vandencourt." He looped an arm around the woman's trim waist. "This is my wife, Susan."

"Lily Michaels."

"Girls, don't wander too far," the woman called.

"We won't!"

Cal smiled at Lily. "They're anxious to stretch their legs a bit. We've been in the car for hours."

Their daughters drifted toward the bird feeder, where a bright-eyed red squirrel was devouring sunflower seeds. The boy attached himself to the man's side and peeked at Lily through the fringe of wheat-blond hair that dipped over his eyes.

"This little guy is our son, Ethan."

Lily squatted down until they were eye to eye. "It's very nice to meet you, Ethan."

"Hi." The boy cast a furtive glance at Missy, who was showing off her good manners by sitting patiently at Lily's feet.

"This is Missy." Lily nodded at the basset hound

and was rewarded with a tentative smile as Ethan bent down to pet the dog.

When she straightened, Cal and Susan Vandencourt were both grinning at each other.

Was she missing something?

"Follow me." Lily motioned the couple toward the shop. "I'll find someone to help out."

"Can we go for a walk, Mom?" The older of the Vandencourt girls pointed to the river. "We'll be careful."

Susan looked at Lily for permission. The moment she nodded, the girls linked hands and dashed away.

"I want to stay with her." Ethan pointed to Missy, who rewarded the boy's loyalty with a swipe of her tongue against his cheek.

Lily had never ventured into the shop before, even though Aiden and Liam had both offered to give her a tour.

"Liam?" She pushed open the door, not quite sure what she would discover on the other side. "There's someone here to see you."

"Cool!" Ethan breathed.

Lily wasn't surprised a boy his age would find the scarred wooden tables, scattered with tools in a variety of sizes and shapes, as intriguing as the toy aisle of a department store.

A door dividing the work area from another part of the building swung open, and the greeting Lily was about to call out got stuck in her throat.

It was Brendan, not Liam, who strode out.

* * *

Brendan saw the smile on Lily's face slip a notch, a dead giveaway she'd been expecting to see one of his brothers.

Too bad he hadn't left when he'd had the chance, but Brendan sensed that Liam needed to get away for a few hours. It was a fair exchange, because *he* happened to need a few hours away from the house.

And Lily.

Brendan had tossed and turned most of the night, a play-by-play of the evening before scrolling through his mind like a digital marquee he couldn't shut off. The tunnel. Lily and her picnic. The three missed calls from Garrett Bridges that had turned up on his phone when they exited the cave, each approximately one minute apart.

The CEO hadn't left a voice mail, but Brendan got the message loud and clear. Bridges wasn't happy that he hadn't been available to finish the conversation.

Because you were deep in conversation with someone else.

Brendan felt a pinch of regret when he remembered the confusion on Lily's face.

How was he supposed to convince Bridges that a small business like Castle Falls Outfitters could handle a partnership with Extreme Adventures when he'd forgotten an important phone call?

Brendan's gaze lingered on Lily's face, searching for evidence that he wasn't the only one who'd had a sleepless night. But no, she looked as fresh and beautiful as her namesake in a white cotton shirt and faded jeans that hugged her slender curves.

"Good morning." Brendan speared his hands into the pockets of his jeans and turned his attention to the cluster of people standing beside her. The couple, dressed like models for an outdoor clothing magazine, looked out of place in the dusty workroom. Their little boy, a carbon copy of his father, was staring up at a canoe suspended from the ceiling, his eyes wide with wonder.

Even though he'd been quite a bit older, Brendan remembered feeling the same way the first time he'd walked into the shop.

Lily took a tentative step forward. "Brendan, this is Cal and Susan Vandencourt and their son, Ethan."

"Hello." The woman's lips curved in a smile. "I hope we didn't tear you away from something important."

"Not at all," Brendan said to be polite.

"We got turned around on one of the roads so it took a little longer to get here, didn't it, honey?"

Her husband didn't respond. He had disengaged from the rest of the tiny group, taking in his surroundings with an intensity that went beyond simple curiosity.

Brendan deliberately stepped into his line of vision. "Welcome to Castle Falls Outfitters."

Cal Vandencourt shook his head. "I just can't

believe it. The place looks exactly the way I remember it."

Brendan's frown deepened. The guy definitely wasn't a local, and he couldn't remember meeting him before. All the orders went through Brendan before they were processed, and he didn't recall seeing their name on an invoice.

"Is there something I can do for you, Mr. Vandencourt?"

"I hope so. I'm looking for Rich Mason."

Brendan's heart buckled under the weight of Cal Vandencourt's expectant smile. A rushing sound that rivaled the falls after the winter thaw filled his ears, drowning out everything else.

"Is he here?"

"No." Brendan felt his throat swell shut. "I…I'm sorry." So, so sorry. "He passed away."

"Passed away?" Cal recoiled as if Brendan had landed a sucker punch to his gut.

"When?" Susan reached blindly for her husband's hand and gripped it like a lifeline.

Brendan's hands fisted at his sides. "About fifteen years ago."

The woman's eyes began to shimmer with unshed tears.

Who were these people?

"I saw the sign by the bridge and thought that Rich… We hoped he was still here." Cal exhaled slowly. "I promised him that I would stop by if I was ever in the area."

I promised. I promised.

The words mocked Brendan. Cut a swathe straight through his heart. Brendan didn't want to answer the questions he saw building in the stranger's eyes like storm clouds.

He'd had to stare down his past in the cave with Lily the evening before and now this.

"I'm sorry this came as such a shock." Lily stepped forward and took control of the conversation, giving Brendan an opportunity to take control over the emotions threatening to spill over the break wall he'd built to hold the memories at bay. "Did you know...Mr. Mason...well?"

Cal blinked rapidly several times. "No."

No?

Brendan couldn't have heard the man right. If that were true, why had the couple had such a strong reaction when they'd learned about Rich's passing?

"Cal and I only spent about three hours with him." A spark of humor kindled in Susan's eyes now, shining through the grief.

Cal's eyes sought Brendan as he tucked his wife closer to his side. "You may not believe this, but Rich Mason saved my family."

Brendan did believe it.

Rich had saved his, too.

"When did you meet?"

Lily was suddenly standing beside him, her hand resting on his arm. Brendan didn't have the strength to move away even if he'd wanted to. Which he didn't.

"Cal dragged me to the Upper Peninsula for our fifth anniversary," Susan's voice was soft, weighted down by memories. "It was the last place I wanted to be."

"Not an outdoor enthusiast?" Lily guessed.

"It didn't have anything to do with location." Susan tilted her head and gave her husband an affectionate smile. "It was the company."

"She means me." Cal's lips twisted. "Our marriage had hit a bit of a rocky spot."

"My suitcases were packed and sitting by the door," Susan said candidly. "Before I could leave, Cal took them hostage and locked them in the trunk of his car."

"Desperate times call for desperate measures." Cal grinned.

"I asked her to go away with me for the weekend. Friday to Sunday. If she still wanted a divorce by the time we got back, I would let her go. She finally agreed.

"We got in the car and I drove north. I had no idea where we were going to end up. The only thing I knew was that I had forty-eight hours to convince the woman I loved to give me a second chance."

Susan chuckled. "About four o'clock in the afternoon, I started to realize that Cal didn't have a destination in mind."

"I was begging God to give me a sign…and all

of a sudden, there it was," Cal continued. "Castle Falls Outfitters. I didn't know what else to do, so I pretended that was our destination all along.

"Rich was standing in the doorway of the shop, almost as if he were waiting for us. We asked for separate canoes, but Rich would only rent us one. We couldn't believe it."

Susan's eyes twinkled. "That's because Cal and I had been arguing the entire way. We were both exhausted and angry and discouraged by the time we got to Castle Falls. At that point, all we wanted was some space. Cal pointed to a whole stack of canoes in the grass and told Rich he'd make more money if he rented two canoes."

"Rich handed each of us a paddle and said it was more important that we learn to work together."

A second lump formed in Brendan's throat. It sounded exactly like something Rich would say.

"We only planned to go out for a little while, but Rich loaded up a tent and camping gear and gave us a few pointers."

"Set a course." Susan lowered her voice several notches in an attempt to imitate Rich's deep baritone.

"You'll get tired but stick with it," Cal chimed in.

"You're a team, not competitors."

"Keep—"

"Your balance," Brendan murmured. The simple bits of wisdom Rich had imparted stirred in his memory.

"You heard it, too." Cal looked pleased. "We didn't pay much attention at the time, because we thought he was coming with us as our guide."

"Instead, Rich sent us out on our own and ordered us not to come back for two days."

Cal planted a kiss on top of his wife's head. "That turned out to be a good thing. Susan refused to talk to me for the first twenty-four hours."

"By the end of the weekend, we both realized there was nothing accidental about seeing that sign by the bridge," Susan said softly. "It was God's plan all along."

"When we got back, Rich was waiting for us. He and his wife invited us for dinner." A cloud passed through Cal's eyes, matching the dark thought that had just occurred to him. "Sunni? Is she…?"

"Still making her famous cinnamon rolls?" Brendan interrupted, quickly putting the man's unspoken fear to rest. "Yes. Every Saturday morning. She happens to be away on a vacation this week."

"It must have been difficult for her to keep the business going," Cal ventured. "I remember Rich saying that he built the canoes and Sunni told him how good they looked when they were finished."

"She still does." A smile somehow slipped past Brendan's internal guard.

Cal studied him for a moment. "Have you worked for Sunni a long time?"

"Fifteen years."

"Fifteen…" A glimmer of recognition flickered in Cal's eyes. "Did you say your last name is Kane?"

"That's right." Brendan didn't like the sudden U-turn in the conversation. It was one thing to listen to the couple share their memories, another to reveal the details of his story.

A smile lit up Susan's face. "God answered Rich and Sunni's prayers, then."

"What do you mean?"

"Rich said they were waiting on the paperwork so they could take in three boys who needed a home. Are you one of them?"

"Yes." Brendan gave a curt nod.

Considering the upheaval Brendan had brought into the Masons' lives, he doubted the couple's prayers had been answered the way they'd expected.

Chapter Fourteen

"What brought you to Castle Falls?"

Brendan looked at Susan, trying to steer the conversation to safer ground.

"After we got our marriage on track again, Cal accepted a job at a company in Colorado. Every summer we take a road trip with the kids and this year, they picked the Upper Peninsula," Susan said.

"They heard us talking about Castle Falls over the years, so here we are. Ethan can't wait to do some fishing and camping..." Cal glanced over at the spot where his little boy had been standing a minute ago.

There was no sign of him.

Susan looked around. "Ethan?"

"I'm in here!"

Brendan pivoted, just in time to see the boy pop up from the bottom of a canoe on display in the corner.

"You can't be in there, sport." Cal was already striding across the room to retrieve his son.

"Is this your canoe, Dad?" The boy didn't seem fazed by his father's reaction.

"I think so." Cal traced his finger along the smooth curve of the bow. "It looks like the one Mr. Mason let me use when your mother and I stopped here a long time ago."

Brendan didn't want to cast a shadow on the man's memories, but he doubted it was the same canoe. This had been the first one Rich had made when he was eighteen years old, a simple design painstakingly fashioned from strips of cedar and canvas. Rich never rented it out to the groups of people who wanted to spend a few hours on the river. Brendan couldn't imagine that he'd made an exception to his own rule and trusted it to a pair of novices like the Vandencourts.

After their foster dad's death, Brendan and his brothers had agreed it should be retired. It now held a place of honor in the shop where Rich had worked, a testimony to a man they'd come to love and admire in the short time they'd known him.

"Out you go, buddy. This canoe belongs to Mr. Kane." Cal shot Brendan an apologetic look as he reached for his son, but the boy shrank back, just out his father's reach.

"I was looking for the tree." Ethan's lower lip began to quiver. "You and Mom said it was there."

"It is," Cal promised. "But you have to ask for permission before you look."

"What tree?" Lily was looking at him for an explanation, but it was Susan Vandencourt who answered the question.

"The one that goes with the verse," she said brightly.

Brendan suddenly understood. They were talking about the logo. The tree and river emblem, along with a reference from the Bible engraved beneath it, were Sunni's design. It was standard issue, and his mother made sure every canoe that left the shop included one of the gold plaques.

"Do you mind?" Cal turned to Brendan. "All our kids know the story."

"Not at all," he said stiffly.

"I'd like to see it, too." Lily was already following Susan Vandencourt, leaving Brendan with no choice but to join them.

"Look! Here it is!" Ethan proudly pointed to a small, rectangular gold plaque fastened to the inside of the canoe.

"*Psalms* 1:3." Lily read the inscription out loud.

"'But his delight is in the law of the Lord, and on his law he meditates day and night,'" Cal quoted. "'He is like a tree planted by streams of water, which yields its fruit in season and whose leaf does not wither. Whatever he does prospers.'"

"That verse saved our marriage," Susan said. "When we got back the next day, we asked Rich what it meant and he pulled out an old leather Bible and read the passage out loud. He said he put the plaque on every canoe he built so he would never forget what was important."

"I'd forgotten," Cal admitted quietly. "I put everything else first, to the point where Susan didn't think I loved her anymore. I decided if the answers were in this book, I'd better start reading it. Rich's verse was the first one I ever memorized."

Rich's verse.

It was the first verse Brendan had memorized, too.

In his mind's eye, he saw Rich holding the canoe steady as Brendan climbed inside. After spending fifteen years surrounded by concrete walls, Brendan had felt equal amounts of terror and exhilaration as they'd started down the river. Rich had followed in this canoe, letting Brendan set the course.

Something he'd been trying to do ever since.

Lily glanced over at Brendan and saw his expression change.

Pieces of the conversation she'd had with Anna Leighton at the ice cream shop began to fall into place. Three boys who had somehow slipped through a crack in the child welfare system. Three boys from Detroit in need of a home.

No wonder they felt like outsiders in a town the size of Castle Falls.

With a different last name than Sonia's, Lily had assumed Brendan and his brothers were part of a blended family.

The flash of raw grief in Brendan's eyes when Cal

had inquired about Rich Mason hinted at a close relationship, but while Brendan referred to Sonia as Mom, Brendan had never mentioned his foster father.

She leaned in for a closer look at the plaque. It was scratched and scarred and the gold plate had worn off the edges. The letters in the verse were crooked. The outline of a tree and the gentle curve of the river looked as if they'd been engraved in the metal with a pocket knife. And yet its very simplicity somehow made it…beautiful.

"Are we going soon, Dad?"

The door burst open and the Vandencourts' daughters bounded into the shop.

"In a few minutes," Cal promised. He reached for Ethan and set him down on the floor next to the canoe. "Why don't you girls get the cooler out of the car while Mr. Kane and I get everything ready?"

"Okay!" The girls disappeared through the door as quickly as they'd come.

Lily glanced at Brendan for an explanation and noticed that he looked just as confused as she was.

"Ready?" he repeated.

Cal flashed a boyish grin. "For our trip down the river."

"We're gonna go exploring." Ethan told Brendan, his initial shyness replaced by anticipation. "We brought a tent and sleeping bags and everything."

"Everything is right." Susan laughed and ruffled her son's hair. "I just hope the canoes stay afloat."

Brendan's brows pulled together in a frown. "You want to put in here?"

"Of course." Cal looked surprised by the question. "Unless you have another group scheduled this morning?"

The question hung in the air, suspended by the sudden silence that swelled between the two men.

"We're sorry." Susan must have drawn her own conclusion from Brendan's expression. "We were so excited, we didn't think to call ahead and reserve the canoes."

"I'm afraid we don't rent canoes anymore," Brendan said. "There are...liability...issues."

There were issues, all right, Lily wanted to say. But she seriously doubted they had anything to do with liability!

"Oh." Cal struggled to hide his disappointment. "Since you kept things going, we assumed that part of the business hadn't changed."

Brendan's shuttered expression hinted there'd been more changes than that when he'd taken over.

"You said I could paddle the canoe, Dad!" Ethan wailed.

Susan and Cal looked at each other, unsure what to do with the unexpected news—and their son's obvious distress.

"There's another place about forty miles from here," Brendan said. "They rent canoes and kayaks."

The couple exchanged a look and Lily interpreted

the silent message that passed between them. It wouldn't be the same.

The Vandencourts wanted more than a few hours on the river; they wanted *this* river.

"Then we'll buy the canoes," Cal declared.

"Buy them?" Brendan echoed.

"That's a great idea." The sparkle in Susan's eyes had returned.

"You don't have a trailer," Brendan said slowly. "What do you plan to do with the canoes when you're done?"

Lily wanted to step on the man's foot. Was he actually trying to discourage a sale?

"We'll have you ship them to the Bible camp our children attend every year," Cal said. "They're always appreciative of donations."

"That depends, of course, on whether you have some that aren't spoken for." Susan flicked a cautious look at her son, unwilling to get his hopes up again.

"We do!" Lily stepped forward, unable to remain silent a minute longer.

Brendan's brows shot up into his hairline.

"*He* does," she amended quickly. "They're a little larger than a standard canoe, though." She winked at Ethan. "With plenty of extra space for camping supplies."

"Perfect," Cal declared. "We'll take them."

Brendan looked at Susan, who was nodding in agreement. "You want to buy two canoes?"

"No." Cal shook his head. "We'll need four. The girls learned how to canoe at camp last summer, so they insisted on having their own this time."

"Four." Brendan still looked shell-shocked, as if he couldn't quite believe this was really happening. "I…happen to have that many ready to go. Come on, I'll get you set up."

Lily hid a smile.

You are so amazing, Lord.

The moment her prayer took wing, another one followed. That Brendan would realize this wasn't simply a case of good timing.

It was *God's* timing.

Brendan didn't have to look at Lily to know that she was smiling. And if she'd had her pom-poms, Brendan also knew there would be a replay of the shuffle he'd seen at the soccer game.

Four canoes.

He still couldn't wrap his mind around it.

"I'll back up the trailer so we can load them," Brendan murmured. He needed a few minutes alone.

Why had he sent Liam to pick up supplies that morning? If Brendan had gone instead, he wouldn't have had to deal with the Vandencourts. Or the past.

Bile began to churn in Brendan's stomach, the same thing he'd experienced when Sunni first told him about Rich's heart attack. Brendan hadn't wanted to face his foster dad, but Sunni said Rich was asking for him.

Brendan had entered the hospital room and felt his

own heart splinter at the sight of Rich lying in the narrow bed, hooked up to tubes that were hooked up to machines. Always robust and larger than life, under the flicker of the fluorescent overhead lights and the heart monitor's digital eye, his foster dad appeared gaunt and pale.

Brendan lingered in the doorway, afraid to see the look of anger or disappointment on Rich's face. Knowing he deserved both only made it worse. What he didn't expect was the smile that flared in Rich's eyes, pulling Brendan to his side like a tractor beam.

He'd reached out and taken Brendan's hand in a surprisingly strong grip.

"Sunni...tell her...means everything to me." The words were faint as Rich's strength advanced and retreated with each fractured breath. "Finish what we started...promise."

Brendan had almost strangled on the lump rising in his throat.

"I promise."

The words had continued to play through Brendan's head as Rich slipped into a coma only a few hours later. In the days following the funeral, they'd become etched in Brendan's heart.

Test results revealed a condition that had caused a slow but potentially lethal deterioration in one of the main valves in Rich's heart, but Brendan knew the truth. Rich's death was *his* fault.

He'd found a letter from Rich's doctor, open on

the coffee table after Sunni had gone through the mail. And even though Brendan hadn't been able to decipher all the medical terminology, near the end of the report he'd read that stress could have been a contributing factor in the heart attack. In the hours before Rich had been rushed to the hospital, Brendan could pinpoint only one thing that might have caused a spike in his foster dad's stress level. Brendan's arrest for trespassing and criminal damage to property.

He felt a tug on his arm and the shadows fled, chased to the corners of his memory by Ethan Vandencourt's gap-toothed grin.

"I'm going to see the wishing well. It's a special place in the river where the water is really calm." He followed Brendan out the door, sabotaging his plan to be alone and talking a mile a minute about their upcoming adventure. "Have you ever seen it?"

"A long time ago." The swimming hole had been a favorite place to spend a lazy summer afternoon with his brothers. None of them had known how to swim when they'd moved to Castle Falls, but Rich had taken them out, one at a time, and patiently taught them the basics.

Brendan fought a sudden, overwhelming urge to retreat to his office. Sequestered there, it was easier to concentrate on the business. To focus on the future instead of the past.

"Why does this canoe have fire on it?" Ethan

was tracing the red flame emblazoned on the side of a canoe leaning against the back wall of the pole building.

"It's my brother Aiden's. His name means 'fiery', so he painted flames on it." He'd also challenged Brendan and Liam to a race down the river that same day. He and Liam decided to humor their little brother, but Aiden was the one who'd had the last laugh. Sunni liked to tease that he had river water, not blood, flowing through his veins.

"Whose is this?" Ethan patted the second canoe in line.

"That one belongs to my brother Liam."

"Oh." Ethan's thin shoulders rose and fell with his sigh. "I have sisters."

Brendan couldn't prevent a smile from slipping out. The Vandencourts' son reminded him of Aiden at that age. "You feel a little outnumbered, hmm?"

Ethan bobbed his head. "Mom says God gives us what we need, but I don't know why He thought I needed *sisters.*"

"Ethan, you aren't bothering Mr. Kane, are you?" His mother rounded the corner, a lifejacket slung over her shoulder like a purse and a bottle of sunscreen roughly the size of a fire extinguisher in her hand.

"Uh-uh." Ethan looked offended by the question. "We're talking about stuff."

"Well, your dad needs someone strong to help him carry the coolers down to the river," Susan said.

"I'm strong!" Ethan bounded away.

"Thank you for being so patient." Susan turned to Brendan with a smile. "You remind me of Rich. You should have seen him trying to teach Cal and me how to paddle the canoe. We went in circles for a while and almost tipped over, but eventually we got the hang of it. I decided Cal and I made a pretty good team after all."

Brendan made the mistake of looking at Lily. She and the girls were playing tag with Missy. Lily's glossy ponytail bounced with every step she took and her smile had the power to warm him from the inside out.

"I know you're probably busy, but we'd love to have you and your wife join us for a few hours," Susan said. "We're planning to set up camp about half a mile down the river and have a cookout."

It took Brendan a moment to realize Susan was talking about Lily. "We aren't…" His tongue threatened to trip over the word. "Married."

Susan didn't look the least bit sorry for her mistake.

"From what I saw, it's only a matter of time." Eyes twinkling, she turned to walk away.

Leaving Brendan to wonder what Susan Vandencourt had seen.

And what life would be like if Lily was here— part of his life. Every day.

Chapter Fifteen

"**D**on't look at me like that." Lily wagged her finger at Missy. "I have permission to be here."

Sonia's permission, but still. Sonia was the one who'd signed the contract with Paint the Town, so Lily was simply checking off the rooms, one by one, on her client's list. And this room happened to be on that list.

The floorboard creaked a warning and Missy, her reluctant partner in crime, whined.

"Shh. It's not an alarm." Although Lily wouldn't put it past Brendan to have a security system hidden somewhere in the room to keep an eye out for trespassers.

After the Vandencourts left on their adventure, Lily spent the remainder of the day choosing the right color for Sonia's bedroom. From the upstairs windows, she'd seen Brendan talking to Liam and Aiden in the driveway. A few minutes later, he'd jumped into his pickup truck and disappeared down the driveway, providing Lily with an opportunity to do a little recon.

Even if Missy didn't approve.

The basset hound flopped down outside the door and refused to budge.

"Fine. You stay here and keep an eye on things." Lily eased into the office, trying to wrestle down the guilt that reared its head as she slipped inside Brendan's office.

By the end of the week, most of the rooms on the list would have a fresh coat of paint. Everything was going according to schedule.

And speaking of schedules…she had to find out how much time she had before Brendan returned.

Lily aimed for the calendar on his desk. It was a good thing Brendan kept track of things the old-fashioned way instead of storing the information in an electronic file. Doing a little pre-makeover surveillance was one thing, but hacking into someone's computer? An activity that definitely fell into the "crossing a line" category.

Although you've already done that a few times, Lily thought ruefully.

Brendan had barely made eye contact with her after she'd introduced him to the Vandencourts. Not that she blamed him.

Every drop of color had drained from Brendan's face when Cal had asked about Rich Mason. For the barest moment, his guard had slipped, long enough for Lily to catch a glimpse of the raw grief simmering below the surface.

No matter the circumstances that had brought Brendan to Castle Falls—and they couldn't have been good if the Kane brothers had been placed in foster care—it was obvious Brendan and Rich Mason had been close.

Lily tried to imagine a younger version of Brendan, shoring up his heart from yet another loss. Compassion welled up, adding to the already confusing mix of emotions that Brendan stirred inside her.

In the cave, she'd sensed a subtle change in their relationship. He'd actually opened up a little. Given her a glimpse into his heart.

And then he'd bolted.

Lily had no doubt Brendan's calendar was somehow to blame. At the moment, however, she was grateful he wrote everything down.

There it was, in black-and-white.

Pick up new generator.

According to the calendar, Lily had approximately twenty minutes until Brendan returned.

Her eyes were drawn to three bright yellow lines that marked off a large segment of time the day before. Six to eight o'clock the evening before. Roughly the same time she and Brendan had been in the cave.

No wonder he'd been in such a hurry to pack up and leave.

He'd forgotten an appointment. Or a…date.

Lily stared down at the initials GB, written neatly on three different lines.

As much as Brendan held himself apart from the people in the community, Lily supposed it wasn't outside the realm of possibility there was someone special in his life. Someone who fit neatly into a square on the calendar and didn't mind being penciled into Brendan's life when it was convenient. Someone he didn't have to sit through a soccer game with or chase through dark tunnels.

In other words, someone that *wasn't* her.

Lily straightened her shoulders and stepped away from the desk. Time to get to work.

The absence of pictures on the walls would make her job easier because there were no holes to patch, and with the technique Sunni had chosen, it shouldn't be difficult to cover up the existing green.

Lily traced her finger along a streak of white where the top coat of paint had been scraped down to the drywall, creating a jagged line that marred the center of the wall like an old scar.

A suspicion began to form and Lily turned to look at Brendan's desk. One of the beveled edges, roughly the same length as the scratch she'd noticed, had been rubbed raw, proof the desk had once faced the window overlooking the river instead of a blank wall.

And even though Lily couldn't prove it, she knew who had rearranged the furniture in the room. What she didn't know was why. The view of the river was breathtaking, a slice of God's creation she could stare at for hours.

Missy whined again.

"There's nothing to worry about. Brendan is—" Lily glanced over her shoulder.

Standing right behind you. She shot a look at Missy. "You were supposed to stand watch."

"She was," Brendan said drily. "She watched me walk right past. Maybe she didn't sound the alarm because this is *my* office."

Lily's cheeks heated. "I wasn't snooping. I was trying to figure out how much time I would need to redo this room."

"I don't like to be interrupted when I'm working."

"And that's why I'm here now." Lily crossed her arms. "When you're *not* working."

Brendan raked his hand through his hair. "How long will it take and what are you planning?"

"Sonia suggested a faux leather finish. It takes a little longer, but the result will be very charming."

"Charming."

Judging from his expression, Lily probably shouldn't have chosen that particular adjective.

"In a manly kind of way," she added.

Brendan laughed.

It was all Lily could do to keep her balance as the walls begin to shrink. She was feeling more like Alice in Wonderland than Nancy Drew.

Brendan had spotted Missy sprawled on the rug outside his office door. A dead giveaway that a beautiful, meddling intruder had invaded his territory, on a mission to change the color of the walls.

Brendan was determined that was the only thing Lily would change during her stay. Her *temporary* stay. A truth he pounded in every time she smiled. Or showed up in unexpected places.

"I can paint the office." Brendan didn't know why he didn't think of that before. "I'm sure Sunni won't mind."

He ignored the little voice inside. The one that said his mother probably *would* mind. Sunni had known exactly what she was doing when she'd hired Lily. She was more interested in matchmaking than makeovers.

The thought wasn't as disturbing as it once was. Something Brendan found even more disturbing.

A sudden commotion outside drew both of them over to the window. Brendan looked outside just in time to see Aiden and Liam, wrestling like otters near the riverbank. Their laughter carried across the yard as they launched two canoes into the water.

Aiden, who quickly took the lead, brought his paddle up and doused his brother. By the time Liam recovered and tried to retaliate, their youngest brother was out of reach.

"He does that every time." Brendan shook his head. "You'd think Liam would try to get a head start. Not that it would do any good. Aiden has mad skills. Rich used to say—" The rest of the sentence locked up in his lungs, trapped by a breath he couldn't expel.

He hadn't meant to talk about Rich, but the Vandencourts' stories had continued to cycle in his mind. Along with the verse he hadn't thought about in years.

His delight is in the law of the Lord...he is like a tree planted by streams of water, which yields its fruit in season.

Cal had looked deeper into Rich's character, searching for the foundation it had been built upon. His faith.

Brendan spent the majority of the day within these four walls, dedicated to continuing the work his foster dad had started but not stopping to consider *why* Rich had started it.

"What did Rich say about Aiden?" Lily prompted softly.

Brendan's gaze snapped back to her. Compassion, not curiosity, glowed in her violet-blue eyes.

"Even the current couldn't keep up with him," Brendan rasped out. "We didn't even know how to swim when we got here. Rich had to teach us how. After that, Aiden spent more time on the water than he did in the house. Liam preferred to hang around and watch Rich in the shop."

"What did you do?"

Brendan could tell by the teasing look in Lily's eyes that thought she knew the answer already. He crunched numbers. But that had come later.

A gifted carpenter, Rich preferred to spend the majority of his time in the shop. He'd made his first canoe for fun, not profit. Whenever he took it out on the river, people asked where he'd purchased it. At Sunni's encouragement, Rich had erected a sign on the road by the bridge and his business had grown by word of mouth. Rich prided himself on the quality of his workmanship and preferred building canoes over balancing budgets.

After Rich's funeral, Brendan had spent weeks sifting through stacks of files, deciphering handwritten notes and trying to make sense of the financial records. That's when he discovered Rich had taken out a second mortgage to cover the rising cost of materials. Sunni had been close to losing the business that Rich had poured his heart and soul into. Sunni had taken them into her home; it had been up to Brendan to make sure she could keep it.

Brendan realized Lily was still waiting for an answer.

"I did what needed to be done," he said simply.

Lily's expression turned pensive. "That isn't always easy."

Brendan remembered what she'd said about expectations and wondered if she was speaking from experience.

"No," he agreed. "Rich liked to say it wasn't navigating the calm part of the river that made you stronger. It was the rapids."

"He must have been an amazing man," Lily finally said.

"He was." Brendan's voice thinned, barely squeezing through the knot in his throat.

"He sure made an impact on Cal and Susan Vandencourt," Lily said. "They gave Rich the credit for saving their marriage, but if you think about it, he really saved an entire family."

Brendan had been trying his best all day *not* to think about it.

He might have found comfort in the stories the Vandencourts had shared if Rich's death hadn't left such a gaping hole in his own life. A hole so deep nothing could fill it. Leaving Brendan with no choice but to build a wall around it instead.

A wall that had come under siege the past few days. About the same time Lily arrived.

A coincidence? Brendan didn't think so.

One more reason to keep her at arm's length.

"Were you and Rich close?" Lily ventured.

"He died of a heart attack about six months after we moved to Castle Falls."

"I'm sorry." Lily's voice was as whisper-soft as the touch of her hand on his arm.

"So am I." Sorry he hadn't had the chance to make up for the trouble he'd caused. Sorry he'd let Rich and Sunni down after they'd generously opened up their home—and their hearts.

"He would be proud of you."

The quiet statement chipped at another layer

of Brendan's fears. How had she known what he was thinking?

Would Rich be proud of him?

Brendan was doing everything in his power to make Castle Falls Outfitters a success. To repay the debt he owed. To keep the promise he'd made.

He turned back to the window in an attempt to put a little distance between himself and Lily—and his memories. Liam and Aiden were almost to the bend in the river, their laughter fading as they paddled out of sight.

"Where are they going?"

Brendan hesitated. "Down the river a little ways."

Lily's eyes narrowed on his face and Brendan resisted the urge to look away.

"You asked them to check on the Vandencourts, didn't you?"

A smile lifted the corners of her lips.

Brendan shrugged. "It's been a while since they've been in a canoe. Besides that, Liam and Aiden never turn down the opportunity to eat a meal they don't have to cook."

"Why didn't you go with them?"

Because I wanted to be with you.

The truth punched Brendan square in the chest, so hard the impact should have sent him crashing into the wall. Not taking a step forward—right into Lily's personal space.

Lily blinked as the space between her and Brendan suddenly disappeared. Her internal circuit board went haywire, thrown off-kilter by the warmth radiating from him.

Her feet melted to the floor.

Lily made the mistake of looking up at him. The flames dancing in Brendan's eyes held her captive.

"Lily—"

Brendan's cell phone broke in, vying for attention.

Lily expected Brendan to step back, but he didn't reach for his phone. He reached for her.

Lily didn't have time to think. Didn't even have time to breathe as Brendan bent his head and claimed her lips in a tender but searching kiss that sent her heart into a free fall. Leaving Lily with no choice but to close her eyes and lean into the protective circle of Brendan's embrace.

The phone started to ring again, and Lily turned her head slightly, breaking the connection.

"It might be something important," she whispered.

"Important." Brendan's gaze roamed over her face, pausing a moment to linger on her mouth, and Lily felt it like a physical touch.

She swallowed hard. "Maybe you should answer it."

Brendan's eyes cleared and he jerked the phone from its holder. "Kane."

Lily decided this was a good time to put some distance between them. Another room. Or county.

"How did you get this number?" Brendan frowned.

Lily started to take a step back but he shook his

head and held up one finger, silently asking her to wait.

"Fine. I'll be there as soon as I can." Brendan hung up the phone. "I'm sorry."

Lily moistened her lips. Sorry the kiss had been interrupted? Or sorry there had been a kiss to interrupt?

"Something that isn't on your calendar?" She strove to keep her voice light.

"A soccer game." Brendan was already halfway across the room. "It starts in fifteen minutes, and Josiah didn't show up."

"They need a coach?"

Brendan tossed a smile over his shoulder.

"And a head cheerleader."

Chapter Sixteen

"We won!"

Lily grinned as several of the players rushed up to her.

Over their heads, she saw Brendan shaking hands with the coach from the other team.

"I think this calls for a celebration." Lily wrapped her arm around Josie's shoulders and gave them a squeeze. "What do you think? Ice cream sundaes at The Happy Cow?"

Noah, a ten-year-old boy who'd been chosen as team captain, shook his head, a mischievous gleam in his clover-green eyes. "We thought of something better."

"Something better than ice cream?" Lily teased. "What would that be?"

Noah looked at Cassie Leighton. Who looked at her sister, Chloe.

Lily sensed a conspiracy.

"My mom said Coach Kane makes canoes," Cassie said.

Coach Kane? Lily did her best to hide a smile. "That's right."

"Does he have a lot?"

Lily thought she knew where this was going. "How many is a lot?"

"Enough for the soccer team," Noah said.

"Before the game, he promised we could do something special if we won," Chloe told her.

"And we won!" Josie said.

"Coach—" Lily caught herself. "Mr. Kane probably had something else in mind." Something that wouldn't take up more than half a square on his desk calendar. But he'd agreed to fill in for Josiah, hadn't he? That had to count for something.

"We'll just tell him we want to take a canoe trip," Noah said. "He won't mind."

Chloe bobbed her head. "We can go this Saturday."

"Er…" Lily tried to think of a way to let them down gently.

"And bring a picnic lunch," Cassie added.

"Hold on a second!" Lily held up her hand, palm facing out, like a crossing guard. "I think we should talk to Mr. Kane before we make any more plans."

"Did someone say my name?"

Lily spun around at the sound of a familiar voice. Brendan was closing the gap between them, a clipboard in one hand and a soccer ball in the other.

His shadow-dark hair had been restyled by the fragrant evening breeze and Lily wasn't even tempted to smooth the unruly strands back in place. The tousled look totally worked for him.

"We were just discussing the victory celebration you promised," Lily managed.

"Ice cream?" Brendan guessed.

"Not exactly." Lily had a sinking feeling he would dismiss the plan the moment it was presented and she hated to see the disappointment on the children's faces. "The team has something else in mind."

Cassie giggled. "Something better."

She and Chloe shifted their position until they stood directly in front of Brendan. The Leighton twins were well aware they had the adorable factor on their side.

Brendan's eyebrows lifted. "And what would that be?"

"Noah, how about you get the team together to pick up the cones while Coach Kane and I talk about it?" Lily suggested.

"Coach Kane?" he murmured as the players obeyed.

"You *are* wearing a whistle."

Brendan anchored the soccer ball loosely against his hip. "So what do they want? Trophies? Their names on the scoreboard?"

"We have a scoreboard?"

"That was going to be my next guess." A small smile tucked in the corner of Brendan's lips.

Lily stared at them a second too long. When she dragged her gaze back to Brendan, the heat in his glance told her that he was remembering the moment in his office, too. A blush started in her cheeks and went all the way to her toes. She crossed her arms over her middle in a vain attempt to protect her heart.

"They want to take a canoe trip. This Saturday. And they want you to be their guide." Lily decided there was nothing to do but lay everything out at once.

"Okay."

"I told them it probably wouldn't work…" Lily stopped. "What did you say?"

"I said okay." Brendan's elusive smile reappeared. "I did promise them a victory celebration. I'll talk to my brothers and see what I can set up."

He strode away, leaving Lily to celebrate a little victory of her own.

Brendan Kane had just made room for life.

A major breakthrough.

Watching him stop to help a pint-size member of the team tie her shoe, Lily's heart swelled almost to bursting…which led her to a major breakthrough of her own.

She wanted Brendan to make room in his life for *her,* too.

"Knock knock."

Liam poked his head through the door, waving

a large white envelope in mock surrender before entering Brendan's office.

"The mail carrier dropped this off a few minutes ago."

"Thanks." Brendan reached across the desk and plucked the envelope from his brother's hand. One look at the return address stamped in the corner and the air emptied from his lungs.

After missing Garrett Bridge's call on Sunday evening, he hadn't heard from the CEO all week. No phone calls. No emails.

Nothing. Now out of the blue, a letter?

Liam frowned. "Everything okay?"

"Sure." Unless the envelope contained a polite form letter, thanking Brendan for his time but letting him know that Extreme Adventures had decided to contract with someone else. Someone who didn't forget an important conference call.

"Aiden and I got the canoes ready. You should be all set for tomorrow morning." Liam strolled over to the window and stared at the river as if he had all the time in the world.

That's why Brendan's desk faced the wall. No distractions.

"Thanks." Brendan's fingers twitched as he set the envelope on the desk.

"What time will the team be here tomorrow?" Liam asked.

"Nine." Brendan hoped the one-word response would push his brother out the door.

But, no. Liam turned to study him and Brendan saw the questions in his eyes. Questions like why, after turning down multiple requests to get involved with New Life Fellowship over the years, had Brendan volunteered to coach the church youth soccer team? And not only that, agreed to take that team on a canoe trip?

Brendan scowled. "I couldn't exactly say no."

"Really?" Liam's mild response was a direct contrast to the defensive edge that sharpened Brendan's tone. "You never seemed to have a problem with that before…." He left the sentence dangling in the air between them.

Brendan silently filled in the blank.

Before Lily.

After Rich died, this room had become his refuge. A place where he could shut out the rest of the world. Every attempt he had made to keep Lily from invading his space had failed and now she constantly invaded his thoughts.

His gaze slid away from Liam, drawn to the spot where Lily had been standing when he'd discovered her in his office the day before. The spot where he'd kissed her.

The spot where she had *let* him kiss her.

Brendan couldn't stop thinking about that, either.

"They'll only be here a few hours," he heard himself say. "No big deal."

The slight lift of Liam's eyebrows said otherwise, but he was wise enough not to push the issue. "We weren't sure there would be enough life jackets to go around. Aiden scrounged up some extras stashed in the rafters of the garage. I hosed off the spider webs, so they're good to go."

"This created more work for you, didn't it?" Brendan hadn't thought about that when he'd told his brothers about the promise he'd made to the soccer team.

"No worries." Liam shrugged. "It does bring back memories, though."

"I'm sorry." After the Vandencourts unexpected appearance the day before, Brendan knew what it was like to get up close and personal with the past.

"Good memories, not bad," Liam corrected. "I used to enjoy teaching people the basics of canoeing. The expression on their faces when they hit the river for the first time…it was like watching someone open a present on Christmas morning."

Brendan had never thought of it that way. "You never said anything."

"You never asked." Liam's easy smile took the sting out of the words.

So why did Brendan feel the need to apologize all over again?

It had never occurred to him that his brothers might have wanted to weigh in on the decision he'd made. Guilt nipped at Brendan's conscience as he looked down at the envelope in front of him.

All the plans he'd made over the years had been in the best interests of his family. Including this one.

"Do you want me and Aiden to go along?" Liam was saying. "Or will you and Lily be able to handle everything?"

"I'm not sure Lily is going with us."

"Why not?"

Because Brendan hadn't asked her.

"She might have other plans." Brendan took evasive maneuvers. "Sunni will be back at the end of the week and in case you haven't noticed, Lily still has a lot of painting to do."

"I think you're the only one who hasn't noticed there's a beautiful woman living in the house."

Brendan shifted in his chair. Oh, he'd noticed all right.

"There's nothing going on between me and Lily."

"Uh-huh." Liam didn't look convinced. "I've got a few things to do. I'll leave you alone with your delusions… Oops. I meant to say thoughts."

Brendan ripped open the envelope the moment the door closed and a thin stack of paperwork slid onto his desk.

A contract.

Brendan could hardly believe it. Garrett Bridges must have dealt with the marketing department's concerns in order to push the contract through.

Here it was, in black-and-white. The fulfillment of the promise he'd made to Rich—and to himself.

Brendan settled back in his chair and began to read.

At first glance, it appeared to be a standard contract, outlining the number of canoes that Castle Falls Outfitters would provide and the deadlines for their arrival.

It would be challenging, but Brendan had no doubt they could keep up with the demand…he frowned when a clause near the end of the contract snagged his attention.

Castle Falls Outfitters will remove the company's logo from every canoe built for Extreme Adventures.

Brendan read it again.

Remove their logo? Where had that come from?

Garrett had never mentioned it when they'd hammered out the details of the contract. The gold plaque with Sunni's emblem, along with the reference from *Psalms* 1, defined their brand.

Brendan reached for his phone and punched in the CEO's number.

The bells above the door jingled as Lily walked into The Happy Cow.

Rebecca Tamblin waved to her from a table in the corner. "Over here!"

Several women, some Lily recognized from the soccer game earlier in the week, turned to smile at her. One of them was Anna Leighton, who scooted down to make room.

"I hope you don't mind meeting here today." The pastor's wife's warm smile encompassed everyone seated around the table. "The children's ministry is having a special event at the church, and they asked if our book group could get together somewhere else this morning."

"Meeting at the ice cream shop?" One of the women teased. "I'm surprised we didn't think of it sooner!"

Anna reached for the carafe and poured Lily a glass of iced coffee. "I like being on this side of the counter once in a while."

"I took some video of the game yesterday," Lily murmured. "I thought you might like to see your girls in action."

"That was so thoughtful of you." Anna's smile made Lily glad she'd thought of it. "I'm hoping to make the next one. Chloe and Cassie can't stop talking about the canoe trip. I had to convince them to wait until tomorrow morning to pack their lunches."

"Are you going along?" Rebecca asked.

"I don't think so." Lily kept her smile in place. "I'm not officially part of the team."

"From what I saw, you're officially part of something," Josie's mother declared.

To Lily's chagrin, knowing smiles passed around the table.

"My husband and I couldn't believe it when Brendan Kane agreed to fill in as coach." This from Noah's mother. "He didn't participate in any sports in high school. In fact, I'm not sure he got involved in anything."

"Except trouble," a woman at the far end of the table muttered.

There it was again, Lily thought. Another veiled reference to something in Brendan's past, like a smear on the lens of a microscope.

Whatever had happened, Lily suspected it distorted Brendan's perception, as well.

"Brendan is really busy, but he cleared his calendar to keep a promise to the team." Lily rose to his defense, hoping they would see another side of him.

In the past twenty-four hours, Lily certainly had.

The strategy backfired. If anything, her comment only made the women's smiles—and their assumptions regarding her and Brendan's relationship— grow larger.

Fortunately, Rebecca took pity on Lily and redirected the conversation by picking up her book. "Time we get started, ladies. Let's turn to chapter two and read the quote at the top of the page."

With an inward sigh of relief, Lily settled into the lively discussion that followed. At the end of the hour, it felt as if she'd known Rebecca Tamblin and her friends for years.

Lily glanced at the clock after the pastor's wife closed their time together with a short but heartfelt prayer. So far, so good. By the time she returned to the house, the baseboards Lily had painted would be dry.

"Lily?" Anna intercepted her at the door. "Do you have a minute?"

"Of course."

"I know you're busy with Sunni's house, but I

wondered if you could take a look at the upstairs," Anna said. "It needs a little work, but I have no idea where to start."

"I can try," Lily said cautiously, not sure what kind of advice Anna was looking for.

"Great. It's something I've been meaning to do for a few years, but I just haven't found the time to tackle another project."

Lily wasn't surprised. She didn't know how Anna juggled a business and a sweet but precocious set of twins.

"Ignore the mess." Anna led Lily to the back of the dining room, where a short hallway opened to a staircase leading to the second story. "At the moment, I use the space for extra storage and it also doubles as my craft room."

Lily's mouth dropped open when she followed Anna upstairs. Staying true to its whimsical name, the ice-cream shop had a charming but rather kitschy decor. This spacious room, with its tin-punched ceiling, gleaming hardwood floor and exposed brick walls, was like taking a step back in time.

Anna yanked the heavy drapes aside and morning sunlight flooded the room. "I want to add more tables and create another dining area up here. More tables mean more room for paying customers."

Lily paused next to a wooden table, drawn to its unusual centerpiece. Silver necklaces, dripping like tinsel from a bouquet of willow branches arranged in a large metal vase, caught her eye. "You make jewelry?"

"The supplemental income I mentioned." Anna fanned away a cloud of dust motes suspended in the air. "Every little bit helps."

"These are beautiful!"

"Thank you." Anna looked pleased by the compliment. "I've never had any formal training, but it's a great way to reduce stress."

Lily picked up one of the necklaces and studied the intricate design. Real leaves and flowers were perfectly preserved in each glass pendant; the gold clasps fashioned to resemble tiny acorns. "Do you have a website? My friend, Shelby, would love one of these."

Anna's burst of laughter answered the question. "Nothing so fancy, I'm afraid. Most of my sales are through word of mouth. Someone sees a neighbor or cousin wearing a piece of my jewelry and orders one for a birthday or anniversary."

Hands on her hips, Anna turned to study the bare wall.

"What do you think of a mural? I managed the polka dots myself but I'd like something a little different up here."

Lily agreed with the assessment. She reached out and traced her finger across the exposed brick as an idea began to take shape.

"First of all, I wouldn't be so quick to turn this space into a second dining room," she said slowly.

"Oh." Anna's face reflected her disappointment. "I was hoping all the room needed was a little sprucing up. You think it would be too much work?"

"No…I think you should convert this space into a jewelry store instead."

"A jewelry store…" Anna's voice trailed off but her eyes took on a warm glow.

Lily recognized hope when she saw it—and it was all the incentive she needed to continue.

"You said you were looking for something that would bring customers in year round. This could be the answer," Lily told her. "You could even offer special evening or weekend hours so people can observe an artist at work in her studio."

"Do you really think so?" Lily could tell by Anna's expression the woman had never considered her jewelry making an art.

"The customers would eat that up." Lily's eyes sparkled. "No pun intended." She'd created marketing plans for several exclusive boutiques in the Chicago area and no one carried a line of jewelry as unique as the pieces Anna had designed.

Anna's gaze swept around the room and Lily could tell she was seeing it through different eyes. When she turned back to Lily, she was smiling.

"When can you start?"

"Start?" Lily squeaked.

"The renovation," Anna clarified. "I want to hire you."

"I'm not…" A custom painter? Staying in Castle Falls?

Both statements would have been true.

So why did she feel a deep longing to be part of this community?

In the past week, without Lily even realizing it was happening, little things had wrapped around her heart, tethering it to Castle Falls. The bone-deep contentment Lily felt whenever she heard the wind shimmy through the trees or watched the sunlight dancing on the river.

The way her pulse leaped whenever Brendan smiled.

Little things adding up to feel like…home.

"I'm sorry," Lily heard herself say. "I can't."

It was better to face the truth than give false hope. For Anna…and for herself.

Chapter Seventeen

"Where's Coach Kane?"

Chloe and Cassie Leighton moved into formation, forming a petite but impenetrable wall that stopped Lily in her tracks as she made her way down to the river.

That, Lily thought, was a very good question. Too bad she didn't have a very good answer.

"I'm sure he'll be here soon." She pasted on a smile, hoping it were true. "There are always a few last-minute details that need attention."

Last-minute being the keywords.

The players had shown up en masse at the specified time, toting life jackets and insulated lunch bags down to the river. Ready for adventure.

The only thing missing was their guide.

Lily had been up since dawn, brewing a fresh pot of coffee and baking blueberry muffins for anyone who'd been too excited to eat breakfast at home, but Brendan had yet to make an appearance.

She'd thought about knocking on the door of his cabin, but decided that would fall into the pushy category.

Kind of like inviting yourself along on a canoe trip.

Lily flicked the pesky thought aside.

So Brendan hadn't *formally* asked her to accompany them.

But he had made it clear he considered her part of the team when he'd taken Josiah's place at the last minute.

When Lily had called Shelby the night before, she'd told her friend how Brendan had filled in for the team's missing coach and agreed to a special outing on the river. And even though Lily left out the moments leading up to the phone call—and Brendan's heart-stopping kiss—somehow her friend had read between the lines.

"It sounds like someone has changed her opinion," Shelby had teased.

Lily couldn't deny it. She'd changed her opinion because of the change she'd seen in Brendan.

A burst of laughter pulled Lily's attention to the riverbank, where a group of parents who'd volunteered to come along as chaperones were gathering. They looked as excited as their children about spending a morning on the river. Earlier, she had overheard a couple reminiscing about the trips Rich and Sunni had sponsored and how nice it was that Castle Falls Outfitters was "open for business" again.

Lily wanted to tell them it wasn't the business that was open—it was Brendan. She still didn't know what had happened in his past, but whatever it was, Lily had confidence that God could turn it into something good.

It was part of the promise.

"Hey, Coach!"

Noah's voice rose above the buzz of conversation.

The knot in Lily's stomach loosened. Until that moment, she hadn't realized how nervous she had been about Brendan's mysterious absence.

"Good—" Morning.

The sentence faded away, along with Lily's smile. Instead of his usual jeans and a T-shirt, Brendan wore khaki slacks and a button-down shirt.

Lily was suddenly face-to-face with a stranger. "You look a little overdressed for a day on the river."

Before Brendan could open his mouth, Lily knew what he was going to say. "Lily, I—"

"You're not going with us."

His curt nod confirmed it. "Something came up. I have to go out of town."

"You mean you're *choosing* to go out of town." Because with Brendan, business came first. How could she have forgotten that?

You wanted to forget, an inward voice chided. *You wanted him to see beyond the four walls of his office. You wanted him to see...you.*

"I'm sorry." Brendan glanced at his watch, obviously eager to be on his way.

Out of the corner of her eye, Lily saw the players standing beside the canoes, their expressions curious but hopeful as they waited for Lily and Brendan to join them.

"You promised," she whispered.

"Aiden and Liam will go along." A muscle tightened in Brendan's jaw. "They're better at this sort of thing than I am, anyway."

Somehow, the excuse hurt more than his apology. Because Lily could see he believed it.

"I'm sorry things didn't turn out the way you'd expected."

Aiden appeared at Lily's side as she dragged her canoe onto the sandy beach. Several of the parents had arrived first and were already unpacking, looking sunburned and damp but somehow refreshed from their excursion down the river.

Shrieks of laughter drifted on the breeze as the children hopped out of their canoes and splashed each other in the shallow water. Ordinarily, the sound alone would have lifted Lily's spirits—if she hadn't been weighted down by Brendan's decision to skip the outing.

"It's not your fault." She scraped up a smile. "I'm glad you and Liam were free today."

At least the other two Kane brothers had their priorities straight.

"It's not Brendan's fault, either."

Aiden's quiet statement stirred up myriad emotions that had been churning inside Lily all morning, but it was anger that rose to the surface.

"Brendan had a prior commitment with the soccer team. He chose to work today instead," she reminded him.

Aiden raked a hand through his hair, a gesture identical to one she'd seen Brendan make when he was frustrated. Under different circumstances, it would have made Lily smile.

"What do you know about our mother?" he asked.

The abrupt change in topic caught Lily off guard.

"You moved to Castle Falls from Detroit," Lily said cautiously. "Sunni and her husband, Rich, were your foster parents."

"Not Sunni...our biological mother."

"Brendan hasn't mentioned her."

"I don't remember much about her. Other than the fact Mom stayed out half the night and slept most of the day.

"Brendan was afraid we'd get taken from our home and split up, so he took care of us. There was a soup kitchen a few blocks away and he'd sneak into the supply room when the volunteers were busy. He figured they were giving away the food, anyway, so it wasn't really stealing. Only one time, he got busted by a volunteer."

"Rich?"

Aiden nodded. "He and Sunni were in Detroit that week with the mission committee from New Life Fellowship. Brendan took off when Rich confronted him, but he and Sunni showed up at our door the next day and invited us to a sports camp the church was hosting.

"Bren was furious, but he gave me and Liam permission just to get us out of the house. It was payday at the factory, which meant Mom would probably drag home some guy after shift change."

Lily winced as a picture of what life must have been like for Brendan and his brothers began to form in her mind.

"Sunni and Rich were only in the city for a week, but they spent the majority of their time with us. Bren didn't trust them, of course, but when he looked at the options, home or church, he chose the place where we could run off our energy and eat a meal that wasn't buttered noodles."

"Didn't Brendan go with you?"

"No." Aiden chuckled. "He can be pretty stubborn, but it turned out the Masons had a secret weapon."

"What was that?"

"They cared about us," Aiden said simply. "We didn't know it at the time, but they'd already contacted a social worker about becoming emergency foster parents. Mom had started drinking heavily, so they knew it was only a matter of time before we were taken out of the home. The day before they left, they asked Brendan about moving to Castle Falls.

"Liam and I wanted to go. Rich had told us about their house on the river and we couldn't wait to see it. Brendan wasn't sold on the idea, but he wanted me and Liam to have a chance at something better."

"It must have been quite a change," Lily murmured. "For all of you."

"It was harder on Brendan. He got off to a...rocky start at school." A shadow passed through Aiden's eyes. "And after Rich passed away, there were a few tough years. Brendan was the one who turned things around."

Lily pulled in a slow breath and let it out. "Why are you telling me this?"

For the first time since they'd met, Aiden didn't respond to one of Lily's questions with a wink or teasing comment.

"Brendan is so focused on the business, it might seem like he doesn't care. It's just the opposite, Lily. He acts that way because he *does*."

Brendan glanced at the rocks outlined by the swirling water below him.

One misstep and down he'd go.

Kind of ironic, under the circumstances.

He gripped a stone jutting out from the rock wall and hauled himself up, hoping it would hold.

One step at a time.

The thought came from somewhere deep inside himself, and Brendan obeyed without thinking until he made it to the top of the falls.

The last time he'd climbed this wall, he'd been looking for Lily. Now he was trying to avoid her.

When Brendan had pulled into the driveway, lights glowed in the kitchen window.

Brendan figured he was going to get a lecture from his brothers the moment they realized he was home, so he'd decided to make himself scarce for a while.

He wasn't planning to end up at the falls, it just happened.

He could still see the expression on Lily's face when he'd told her that he wasn't going on the canoe trip.

Brendan wanted nothing more than to pull her aside and explain everything, but there hadn't been time.

Garrett Bridges had returned Brendan's phone call at ten o'clock the night before. He was in Detroit for the weekend and offered to meet with Brendan in person to talk about the amendment to the contract.

An offer Brendan couldn't afford to refuse, especially when a partnership between Castle Falls Outfitters and Extreme Adventures was at stake.

The explanation Brendan had been hoping would put his mind at ease had only left him feeling more unsettled.

He bent his head and stepped through the curtain of water. After hours in the car, the spray of water felt cool against his skin but did nothing to refresh his soul.

God...

It was the start of a prayer Brendan didn't even

know how to finish. Which told him that his relationship with the Creator wasn't as close as it should be.

When he reached the narrow spot in the tunnel, Brendan's thoughts automatically turned back to Lily.

Stuck in a quandary.

He'd chuckled at what he'd thought was a humorous way to label her situation, but now he understood all too well what that felt like. Whether to turn around or keep moving forward, into the unknown.

Brendan squeezed through the opening, guided by a soft glow that illuminated the path ahead. A light that didn't extend from the beam of his flashlight, but came from something inside the cave.

Someone was already there.

The steady drip of water from the sandstone ceiling sounded louder, magnified by the silence as Brendan hesitated.

One of his brothers? Or a hiker who'd ignored the no-trespassing signs and stumbled upon the opening of the cave?

Or the one person who had worked her way into his life...and his heart.

"Marco."

Brendan tossed out the word and waited.

"Polo."

The soft response reached out from the gloom and grabbed Brendan by the heart and carried him forward. He reached the opening to the cave and there she was, sitting cross-legged on a blanket.

Packing up to go.

"I'm sorry." Lily refused to look at him as she stuffed an insulated cup into her backpack, recreating a scenario similar to the one that had played out between them the last time they were in the cave. "I didn't realize you would be here...."

Or I wouldn't be.

Brendan filled in the blank, knowing he deserved it.

Suddenly, being alone with his thoughts wasn't so appealing.

"Lily...wait."

"Why?"

The uncertainty in Lily's voice, the absence of her smile, told Brendan he'd damaged something precious.

"I want to explain."

"Okay." Lily still looked wary but Brendan detected a quiet invitation embedded in her sigh.

"About six months ago, the CEO of a large sporting-goods chain contacted me about forming a partnership."

Lily's audible gasp made Brendan smile.

"That was my reaction," he admitted. "The flagship store is located in Minneapolis and there are four more scattered throughout the Midwest. The potential for growth is phenomenal."

"It sounds like a great opportunity."

Brendan nodded. "A contract like the one they offered means financial security. The work will be year-round instead of waiting for orders to trickle in. We've been hammering out the final details, trying to come to an agreement, and yesterday the contract came in the mail."

"But it wasn't what you expected."

"No." Brendan was no longer surprised at Lily's perceptiveness. "Somewhere along the line, they added a clause, stating we agreed to remove the *Psalms* 1 logo from all the canoes sold in their stores. A little detail that somehow slipped through the cracks during negotiations. I met with him today to talk about the change."

Lily's eyebrows dipped together. "Did you sign it?"

"Not yet."

"Then it must not be a little detail."

Chapter Eighteen

Lily hadn't raised her voice but Brendan's head snapped back, the impact of the words like an upper cut to the jaw.

"It's not an unreasonable demand," he shot back. "I'm not sure how many of our customers even notice—or care—about the logo. It's not like it has any significance outside of the family."

"Cal and Susan Vandencourt don't think so."

A one-two punch.

"When it comes to business, you can't be sentimental," Brendan argued. "Let your emotions get in the way."

Lily's fingers knotted together in her lap. "From the things I've heard about Rich Mason, I'm not sure he would agree."

Brendan wished he hadn't said anything.

If Lily instinctively knew the things he had been grappling with since he'd read that clause, why didn't she realize Rich was the reason he wanted the business to succeed?

"Rich made every canoe to order. You can't run a business that way anymore. Things change." And Brendan had the financial records to prove it. "All we'd be doing is removing a plaque from some of the canoes."

The tiny frown between Lily's brows deepened as she absorbed the words. "So Liam and Aiden don't have a problem with it?"

Brendan shifted under the weight of the guilt that pressed down on his conscious. "I haven't told them yet."

"They don't know about the clause?"

"They don't even know about the initial offer," Brendan admitted.

Until a few hours ago, Lily would have labeled Brendan's actions arrogant or controlling. Now, thanks to Aiden, she understood he had been hard-wired from childhood to protect his brothers.

Lily had sought out a quiet place where she could begin to sort through her troubled thoughts following the conversation with Aiden. She hadn't expected her sanctuary to be disrupted by the six-foot two, blue-eyed man responsible for those thoughts!

The moment she'd heard his voice, Lily's pulse spiked like a seismograph that detected a sudden disturbance below the surface of the earth.

She'd been ready to paint Brendan's office walls cotton-candy-pink when he'd bailed on the canoe trip that morning. But that was before Lily had pieced together a picture of Brendan's home life in Detroit and realized what motivated him.

"But...don't they have a say in what happens?" Lily couldn't help but ask. "It's their business, too."

"They've always left decisions like this up to me." Brendan paced a restless circle around the cave, propelled by whatever thoughts continued to nip at his heels. "I didn't want to get everyone's hopes up and then have the deal fall apart at the last minute. Which could still happen if I refuse to sign the contract. According to the CEO, marketing made the recommendation, and he said the company defers to their experience in matters like this."

And in Lily's experience, the CEO was simply passing the buck.

"Some of the parents who went with us on the canoe trip today were reminiscing about Rich," she said carefully. "He built canoes but it was more than a business. He treated it like a ministry. Invested in people's lives."

"What do you know about it?" Brendan skidded to a stop and turned to look at her, his eyes shooting sparks of blue fire.

Lily refused to be intimidated by his scowl. "Cal remembers Rich as a man who obeyed God. Looked to Him for direction."

"If I let this opportunity pass, there might not be another one."

It sounded to Lily as if Brendan wasn't trying to

convince only her, he was trying to convince himself. He might assert there was no room for emotion in a business transaction, but the turbulence in his eyes belied the statement.

Aiden had spoken the truth. Every decision his older brother made welled from a deep sense of responsibility, even if it didn't always appear that way on the surface. Was it any wonder, then, the clause in the contract was eating him up inside? Another man—a man like her father—would have signed on the dotted line without a second thought.

"Sometimes a logo is more than the name of the business or an eye-catching marketing technique." Lily sent up a silent prayer that God would give her the right words to say. "It can be a…a touchstone."

"A touchstone."

"What you use to determine the quality of something," she explained. "And it isn't always about numbers. You have to look at the bigger picture."

"That's what I'm doing." Lily almost heard the loud thump as Brendan's walls slammed back into place. "Unless you've been faced with a decision… had to take a risk that could mean the difference between success and failure…you wouldn't understand," Brendan ground out. "Signing the contract is what's best for everyone. The financial security means Sunni won't have to worry about retirement. We'll have the safety net of a major corporation."

Lily wasn't so sure. She knew the way this worked. More than likely, what Brendan viewed as a safety net would become the ties that bound them to someone else's decisions.

"It's a win-win situation."

"If that's true, you wouldn't have met with the CEO today."

Brendan's frustration showed in his eyes as he dropped down on the ground next to her. "I didn't understand why marketing had a problem with our logo. I wanted him to explain it."

"Did he?"

"No." Brendan pulled a leather wallet from the back pocket of his jeans and fished out a business card. "He suggested I call this number on Monday morning and talk directly to the person in charge of their marketing division."

Lily glanced down at the card and the blood froze in her veins.

"Pinnacle?"

Brendan frowned. "You've heard of them?"

"Yes." Lily scraped out the word from a throat that had suddenly gone as dry as dust.

She had a stack of cards exactly like the one in Brendan's hand. Her boss's name and number was printed on the bottom.

"I work for them."

Brendan searched Lily's face—her suddenly *white* face—and felt a cold finger sweep down the length of his spine. "What do you mean, you *work* for them? Did you hire this particular marketing firm to grow your painting business?"

"Paint the Town isn't *my* business. My best friend started it a few years ago." Lily pushed to her feet, and for a moment, Brendan thought she was going to bolt for the entrance of the cave.

An image of Lily closing her laptop, trying to hide the tutorial she'd been watching, flashed in his mind. Brendan had assumed she was new to the custom-painting business. It had never occurred to him that Lily might not *be* a custom painter.

"I think you'd better explain." The business card crumpled in his hand.

"Shelby was diagnosed with Lyme disease in the spring and the side effects made it impossible for her to work. Nausea. Extreme dizziness. She's self-employed and didn't have anyone to fill in for her. I took a leave of absence from my job to help out until she got back on her feet."

"Is she getting better?"

The look of gratitude on Lily's face made Brendan glad he'd asked the question.

"The disease got quite a foothold before the doctor finally figured out what was wrong, but he's optimistic she'll make a full recovery."

"So you came to her rescue." It fit Lily's personality. She reminded Brendan of Sunni, always willing to intervene, whether it was finding an overweight basset hound a permanent home or encouraging a soccer team to victory.

Lily locked her arms around her middle, a gesture that struck Brendan as oddly vulnerable.

"Not right away," she said in a low voice. "I knew Shelby was sick, but whenever I made plans to visit her, something at work needed my attention more.

"My boss hinted that I was next in line for a promotion, and I wanted Shelby to celebrate with me. But when I showed up at the door of her apartment to surprise her, she couldn't go. She couldn't even get out of bed. That's how sick she was."

Lily's voice thinned and Brendan understood. He'd felt the same way when he'd walked into Rich's hospital room. Helpless. Angry with himself. And with God.

"I asked Shelby what I could do to help. All she wanted me to do was pray for her." Lily's smile broke. "It sounds pretty simple, doesn't it? But that's when I realized how far I'd drifted away from God. How out of balance my life had become."

"It isn't wrong to work hard," Brendan heard himself say.

"No, it isn't," Lily agreed. "But God knows what it costs us if we give our hearts to anything that isn't *Him*. That's what I'd been doing all along and didn't even realize it. Until I was faced with one those difficult decisions you mentioned a few minutes ago... and the consequences."

"Your father?"

Lily's nose wrinkled. "You remembered."

Brendan remembered a lot of things. "He was worried you would jeopardize your promotion?"

"I think he was more worried I would somehow

jeopardize his relationship with my boss. Pinnacle keeps my father's law firm on retainer." Lily's gaze dropped to her feet. "Shelby protested at first, but I didn't give her a choice. Growing up, she was the one who always trusted God. I heard 'Lily, God will make a way' all the time while we were growing up.

"Finally, I had an opportunity to say the words to her. She stopped arguing and handed over her paintbrushes."

"And a DVD?"

Lily turned pink. "That was my idea. Shelby has a great reputation, and I didn't want to mess anything up. She worked too hard building her business to lose it all because she was too dizzy to climb a ladder."

"Does my mother know you're not a professional painter?" Brendan finally voiced the question that had been nagging him since Lily's confession. Even though he couldn't find fault with the work Lily had done, he didn't want to think she'd lied to Sunni.

"I told Sonia the day she contacted Shelby through the website and inquired about an estimate," Lily said. "I called her back and explained the whole situation. She said from the way it looked, there'd be a 'bushel of blessings' all around. For her and for Shelby."

"That sounds like something Mom would say." A smile nudged at the corner of Brendan's lips. "But what did you get out of it?"

"Knowing I chose the best thing. The right thing."

The words sliced deep. How was he supposed to know what that was?

"You really believe God makes a way?"

"Yes." Lily's gaze didn't waver.

Brendan smoothed the crumpled edges of the card and his thumb grazed the silver mountain peak embossed in the upper corner.

Pinnacle. The logo told him more about what the company stood for than anything he'd find on Wikipedia. Maybe Lily was right. Maybe Bridges and his marketing people would be open to some sort of compromise.

He handed Lily the card.

"Maybe this is it."

Chapter Nineteen

"It's about time you called, Lily. Tell me you're in your office, ready for our nine o'clock meeting with Orion Software."

Lily could picture Dennis Tate in his ergonomically designed leather chair, one hand wrapped around his iPhone, the other his morning cup of java. Lined up on her boss's desk would be a copy of the daily newspaper, a tower of pink antacids and a detailed outline of the clients he would be meeting with that day. Her boss's routine was as predictable as his Thursday afternoon tee time at the country club and he expected everyone who worked at Pinnacle to operate the same way.

Creative, yes. Spontaneous a definite no.

"I'm still in Castle Falls." Staring at a can of paint that didn't look anything like the color on the sample Sonia had picked out. Or maybe it was her vision that was faulty. A sleepless night had a tendency to do that to a person.

Dennis's huff of frustration grated in her ear. "That's what I was afraid of, but your father had me convinced you'd be back where you belonged by Monday morning."

Where she belonged.

A week ago, Lily would have said she belonged in her studio apartment, located half a block from her office so she would be closer to work. But something had changed, so subtly Lily didn't realize it was happening until she'd taken Missy for a walk after church on Sunday morning. The basset had stopped at a fork in the path and looked to Lily for direction. Without thinking, Lily had said, "Let's go home."

The dog had immediately turned to the left and trotted down the path. Right past Brendan's cabin.

Which, of course, had triggered yet another replay of their last conversation.

Lily had barely recovered from the shock of seeing Brendan holding one of Pinnacle's business cards when he'd handed the card to her.

That he had even asked for her help filled Lily with hope. Hope that God had heard her prayers and was working in Brendan's life. And maybe, in a small corner of Lily's heart, hope that somehow she would be part of his future.

Even if it meant inching over the invisible line that separated a boss from his employees.

Lily released a breath she hadn't realized she'd been holding. "Do you have a minute to talk?"

"You aren't going to ask for more vacation time, are you?" Dennis demanded.

"No." Lily didn't bother to remind her boss that she wasn't basking in the sun on a tropical island. "I'm actually calling about one of your clients. Garrett Bridges?"

"CEO of Extreme Adventures. Rising star in the sporting-goods arena. They're planning to open two more stores in the next few years, one in St. Louis and another in Branson." The pride in Dennis's voice was unmistakable, as if he were personally responsible for the chain's success.

The inside of Lily's mouth felt like sandpaper as she forged ahead. "They've been negotiating with Castle Falls Outfitters—"

"A little mom-and-pop joint in the Upper Peninsula," Dennis interrupted. "They should be thrilled they got an offer."

"Garrett Bridges inserted a clause requesting that Castle Falls Outfitters remove their logo from the canoes. Do you happen to know anything about that decision?"

"Of course," Dennis boomed. "It was my idea in the first place."

Lily had been afraid of that. She took another step over the line. "It seems a little—" *Unreasonable? Unfair?* "—unusual. Can I ask why you made the recommendation?"

"A Bible verse on a plaque. Sunday-school stuff," Dennis scoffed. "Fine on the wall of a church, not in a canoe. In my opinion, it's not necessary. In fact, it might turn some people off."

Or change their lives, Lily thought. Like it did for Cal and Susan Vandencourt. And countless others who'd been impacted by Rich Mason's life and testimony.

No. Lily decided that wasn't quite accurate. From what she had discovered, Rich's life and testimony were one and the same.

"Now answer a question for me," her boss demanded. "Why the sudden interest in Extreme Adventures?"

"Castle Falls Outfitters is in Castle Falls. Which is where I've been staying. I've met Brendan Kane, the owner."

"A coincidence that may work in our favor."

Except that Lily didn't believe in coincidences. "What do you mean?"

"I mean you can convince the guy he's making the biggest mistake of his life if he passes up this deal."

"Isn't there a way to compromise?" Lily pressed on, even though she realized she was venturing further into dangerous territory. She'd polished and tweaked some of the ideas her boss came up with but she'd never outright questioned one of them before.

"Extreme Adventures doesn't have to compromise," her boss said bluntly. "If Brendan Kane wants to play in the major league, he's the one who has to bend. Learn to let go."

"Of his values?" Lily bit her lip, but not fast enough to prevent the words from spilling out.

"Values don't pay the bills. If you want to succeed, you do whatever it takes." The hint of steel in Dennis's voice warned Lily what was coming next. "And here I thought you felt the same way."

Lily winced. Past tense.

"You know I'm committed to the company."

"That's good to know. Because we've got a new client flying in from Chicago at the end of the week who specifically asked to work with Lily Michaels. I'll email you the specifics and you can set up a time."

Lily's stomach began to churn. "I won't be back until the weekend. I have to finish up this project."

"*This* is the project that needs your attention. I would hate to have to pass this project on to someone else." Dennis paused to let that sink in. "And Lily? Get Kane to sign that contract."

Dead air signaled the end of the call and Lily closed her eyes.

Brendan wasn't the only with a difficult decision to make.

Brendan turned on the outside faucet, picked up the hose and tried to figure out how he'd gotten stuck with getting the Vandencourts' canoes ready for shipping.

The sound of laughter had preceded the family's

return earlier that morning and Brendan had walked to the window just in time to see Cal and his wife, paddling side by side in bright red canoes, bend toward each other and steal a kiss while their children weren't looking.

Envy cut so deep, Brendan pressed a hand against his chest to make sure he wasn't bleeding.

Sunni and Rich had had that kind of marriage. The shared-smiles and finishing-each-other's-sentences kind. Qualities of a relationship Brendan hadn't had time to pursue—mostly because there hadn't been anyone he *wanted* to pursue.

Until Lily.

The distance would be a factor, but they could see each other on weekends...

Getting a little ahead of yourself, aren't you, Bren?

He brushed aside the question and a series of images flooded in to take its place.

The flash of disappointment in Lily's eyes when his phone rang just when Brendan had kissed her. The warmth in her violet eyes. The touch of her hand.

Whatever was happening between them, Lily felt it, too.

With the Extreme Adventures' contract, Brendan could finally afford to hire a secretary and maybe even some part-time help in the shop to ease the burden on his brothers. For the first time, Brendan felt like he'd proven himself. That he had something to offer.

His lips pursed in a silent whistle, and Brendan suddenly realized the tune playing in his head was the same one he'd heard Rich hum while they worked.

He glanced at the canoe propped next to Aiden's. Spider webs decorated the bow and exposure to the elements had sanded away the shine of the original paint.

Brendan swiped at the cobwebs decorating the bow. No fancy flames on his canoe. He'd given his youngest brother a hard time while he'd worked and Aiden had flicked paint at him.

"You're just jealous because your name probably means grouchy," he'd shot back. "You should paint a bear on the side of your canoe."

Rich had ruffled Aiden's hair. "Brendan's name means navigator."

"Boooooring." Aiden stretched out the word.

Brendan thought so, too, until Rich tossed a wink his way.

"It means to steer a course," their foster dad said. "And that takes faith, skill and determination. Qualities a man needs if he wants to reach his destination."

The words echoed through Brendan's soul.

"I'm almost there, Rich," he murmured.

His head jerked around at the sound of a footfall behind him. Great. All he needed was for one of his brothers to think he was talking to himself. They'd tell Sunni and she'd make *him* go on a cruise.

But it was Lily walking toward him across the lawn.

As always, Brendan felt his pulse kick into high gear. Sunlight sparkled in her hair, flowing loose around her shoulders the way he liked it. Although the ponytails were fetching, too. Paint spattered the front of her shirt and a streak of cinnamon—the same color he'd seen on a paint chip taped to the door of his brother's old room—had ended up on her cheek.

Tenderness welled up inside, an emotion Brendan wouldn't have been able to put a name to before Lily breezed into his life.

She claimed she'd put her career at Pinnacle above everything else, but no matter how hard Brendan tried, he couldn't picture a Lily who didn't make time for ice cream after a soccer game. Or dropping her paintbrush to make a pie for the two scavengers who lived above the garage.

"Brendan—" One look at her expression and Brendan knew she'd spoken with her boss…and what the outcome had been.

"Okay." He breathed out the word. "Thanks for calling him."

"Dennis Tate, my boss, thinks the verse isn't necessary because your name is going to be attached to the canoes. He thinks…it might actually hurt sales."

"Do you agree?"

Lily was silent for so long, Brendan wondered if she was going to answer the question.

"No." Her eyes lifted and held his. "I don't."

Brendan blew out a quiet breath. "It was worth a shot anyway."

"Once Dennis makes a decision, he won't budge. But I could call Garrett Bridges and—"

"No." Brendan didn't want Lily to step any further out on a limb for him. "It will be okay."

"You're right." Lily's smile came out in full force. "There have to be other options."

"The wording is pretty specific." Brendan had read through the contract several times. "I have a few questions for Bridges the next time we talk, but things should go pretty quickly now."

Lily was staring at him as if he'd started speaking a different language.

"What—" her voice lifted a notch "—are you talking about?"

"The contract." What was *she* talking about?

"You're planning to sign it? The way it is?"

"Why wouldn't I?" Brendan couldn't believe Lily had to ask. "It's a dream come true."

"Whose dream?"

Brendan's hands fisted at his sides. "I've been working toward this for fifteen years, Lily. Think about what we'd be giving up."

"That *is* what I'm thinking about," Lily said. "And I think signing the contract would be a…mistake."

"Then it's a good thing the decision isn't up to

you." Anger was the only shield Brendan could use to deflect the disappointment he saw in Lily's eyes. "This is *my* choice."

"You're right," she whispered. "It is your choice." She turned on her heel and fled to the house.

As Brendan watched her disappear inside, he couldn't shake the feeling he'd just made the wrong one.

Chapter Twenty

Lily snapped another picture of the waterfall for Shelby's scrapbook.

She'd almost forgotten the promise she'd made to document her visit to Castle Falls until she'd read Shelby's latest email. Over the past few days, Lily had turned her attention to something she could change—namely the color of the walls—rather than something she couldn't. Like Brendan's decision.

It'll be all right, he had said.

She'd assumed the words meant he'd taken a step forward in faith and planned to continue building on the foundation Rich Mason had started.

Lily had worked in the corporate world long enough to know that a company like Extreme Adventures was all about profit and margin. Castle Falls Outfitters might keep their name, but they would lose their identity. The very thing that set them apart from everyone else.

Why didn't Brendan see it?

He'd given up too easily, in Lily's opinion.

Oh, wait a second. Brendan didn't *want* her opinion. He'd made that clear during their last conversation.

Lily had left before she said something she would regret, and Brendan hadn't followed. Since then, she'd been careful not to cross the perimeters he'd set in place the day she'd arrived in Castle Falls. "Come on, Missy. Let's go back." Lily looped the strap of the camera onto her wrist and began to retrace her steps.

She'd accepted Anna Leighton's invitation to join her and the twins for a pizza-and-movie night. Hopefully, by the time she returned, she would be able to work again without the distraction of knowing Brendan was in his office.

As they neared the house, the snick of a car door brought Missy's nose off the ground. She lifted her nose in the air and it began to quiver like a divining rod, her head slowly turning in the direction of a petite woman crossing the lawn.

"Don't—" Before Lily could finish the thought, the basset hound was off and running.

By the time Lily caught up to her, there wasn't time to shout a warning. Bassett hound and visitor collided. With a cry, the woman sat down hard on the grass. Missy took advantage of the situation and wriggled into her lap.

"I'm so sorry." Lily was apologizing before she reached the woman's side. "Missy doesn't usually act like this with people she doesn't know." She wrapped one arm around Missy and tried to get the dog under control.

"That explains it then!" Brown eyes sparkling with laughter, the woman sprang to her feet and began brushing away the blades of grass clinging to her lime-green Bermuda shorts. "We've already met. I'm Sunni Mason." She extended her hand. "And you must be Lily. It's nice to finally meet you in person."

Lily automatically grasped Sonia's hand. "Brendan wasn't expecting you until tomorrow."

For some reason, Sonia's smile widened.

"I wanted to surprise him." She gave Lily a saucy wink. "Keeps the man on his toes."

"Er…yes." Lily heard herself agree.

Brendan's mother looped her arm through Lily's. "I can't wait to see what you've done to the house."

Lily decided now would be as good a time as any to confess she hadn't quite finished the job she'd been hired for. "Mrs. Mason—"

"Call me Sunni. Everyone does."

"Sunni." Lily found the woman's warmth contagious. "I didn't—"

A loud whoop drowned out the rest of the sentence as Aiden spotted them. He closed the distance between them in three long strides and swept Sunni into his arms.

"I take it you missed me." Sonia laughed, but tears shimmered in her eyes as she hugged her youngest son. "Or did you miss my cooking?"

"I missed you… Lily did a lot of the cooking." Aiden winked at her. "She makes a mean apple pie."

"Is that so?" Sunni glanced at Lily and her smile doubled. "I'll have to get your recipe. How did these blue-eyed hooligans talk you into feeding them?"

"It was no trouble." Lily began to back up as Brendan sauntered out of the house, hands tucked in the pockets of his jeans. Sunglasses shaded his eyes—and his expression. "The house tour. You… We don't…" Lily's sentence began to short out. "I mean, we can always do it later. I'm sure you've got a lot to talk about."

Sunni's gaze bounced between Lily and Brendan. For a moment, Lily was afraid Brendan's mother would insist, but all she did was nod and say, "We certainly do."

"Is that a shark?"

Brendan leaned in for a better look at his mother's camera.

"Just a little one. I don't know why they have such a bad reputation." Sunni waved her hand over the photograph. "He only came within a few feet of our diving group."

Somehow, when Brendan had pictured his mother on a cruise, there'd been more iced-tea sipping and sunbathing than climbing rock walls or swimming in shark-infested waters. But according to the photographs she'd been scrolling through, Sunni had been a willing participant in both.

"It looks like you had a great time, Mom." Aiden's gaze lingered wistfully on a photo of a group standing in front of a zip line. "Maybe I'll get to visit there sometime."

"It would be a wonderful place for a honeymoon."

Brendan realized Sunni was looking at him.

In fact, *everyone* was looking at him.

He flipped to the next picture. "You took a picture of your dessert?"

The magic word. Everyone turned their attention to the swan-shaped cream puff swimming in a pool of chocolate syrup.

Sunni sighed. "The food was wonderful, but I'm going to have to walk dogs at the shelter every day to lose the two pounds I gained."

Missy, who'd been napping at her feet, came to life when she heard the *W* word. Brendan reached down and knuckled the spot between the dog's floppy ears.

Sunni, who didn't miss a thing, smiled at him. "Looks like you made a friend while I was gone."

And lost one, too.

The thought chased through Brendan's mind, churning up emotions he'd tried to ignore.

"Something on your mind, sweetheart?"

Brendan pulled in a breath. "Yes. There is."

"Oh, oh. I know that look."

"I thought we discussed business on Tuesday nights," Liam complained.

"Over pizza," Aiden added.

"This isn't about business...it's about family." Brendan pushed to his feet.

To his astonishment, Liam and Aiden bumped fists.

"It's about time," Aiden crowed.

Brendan frowned. "What's about time?"

Sixty seconds into it, Brendan's brothers stopped smiling.

"Let me get this straight." Aiden's lips barely moved, the grim look on his face masking his usual smile. "You've been negotiating with a major sporting-goods chain for six months and you're finally getting around to telling us about it now?"

Put like that...

Brendan nodded. "I didn't want to get your hopes up."

Aiden leaned forward and slapped his palms against the table. "We aren't six years old, Bren. Liam and I managed to recover when you told us the tooth fairy wasn't real."

"You did take it pretty hard, as I recall." Brendan smiled.

His brother didn't.

Okay, so they were going to be a tough audience. He shouldn't have been surprised, especially after seeing Lily's reaction when he'd mentioned he'd kept his family in the dark about the offer from Extreme Adventures.

"And they want to carry our line of canoes, but they tacked a condition onto the contract." Liam's chair creaked when he crossed his arms and leaned back. "A deal breaker."

"Not necessarily." Brendan glanced at Sunni, who'd remained strangely silent since he'd dropped the bomb on them. Concern shadowed their mother's eyes but he had a hunch it was directed more at him than the situation.

"What do you mean? You have a plan to convince Bridges to reverse the decision?" Aiden asked.

Brendan shook his head. "That's not an option."

There have to be other options.

Lily wasn't in the room, and yet she'd managed to join the conversation. Just the way she'd invaded his life. And his heart.

Liam's eyes narrowed. "You aren't planning on signing it?"

"They're still going to market the canoes under our name," Brendan could see the storm clouds gathering on Aiden's face. "And we wouldn't be removing the logo on all of them. Just the ones for Extreme Adventures. Think about what it would mean. Steady work. Recognition."

Liam shook his head. "It doesn't feel right. It feels like we're selling out."

"We're not selling out...we're selling canoes." Brendan turned to his youngest brother. "Aiden?"

"I agree with Liam. If that counts for anything," Aiden added.

Brendan bristled at the implication.

"It counts," he bit out. "You've never had a problem trusting my judgment before."

"That's because you've never given us reason. But lately—"

Aiden lapsed into silence when Liam shot him a warning look.

"Lately…what?"

"Your judgment stinks," Aiden said flatly.

"I have no idea what you're talking about."

"I'm talking about Lily."

"What about her?"

Aiden smirked at him. "The fact you have to *ask* is exactly why your judgment stinks."

How had the conversation turned from the contract with Extreme Adventures to Lily? That's what Brendan couldn't figure out.

"Why don't we revisit this conversation tomorrow?" Sunni rose to her feet. "It's been a long day and I think I'll turn in for the night. Flip the lights off before you leave and wipe up any blood that gets spilled on the floor. I'll see you all in the morning." She hugged each of them in turn. When she got to Brendan, she whispered in his ear, "You'll make the right decision, Brendan. You always do."

Not according to Lily. Or his brothers.

Brendan folded Sunni into a hug. "'Night, Mom."

The snap of the front door told him that Aiden had already left the building but Liam wasn't as fast.

You have to look at the bigger picture, Lily had said. But wasn't the bigger picture about bringing

Castle Falls Outfitters up to its potential? Making the business Rich had started with one canoe something he would be proud of? Making it a success?

"Liam? Hold on."

It wasn't the hesitation on his brother's face that plowed a furrow straight through Brendan's heart; it was the guarded expression he wore.

Color him confused, but shouldn't they be celebrating now? Cheering instead of slamming doors?

"What's the deal?" Brendan tried not to let his frustration show. "I thought you and Aiden would be more excited about the opportunity. You'll still be building canoes. Doing the type of work you enjoy. What's changed?"

Liam shook his head.

"You have."

"You'll be here tomorrow?"

"That's right!" Lily was glad Shelby wasn't in the room to see her expression and cheerful tone weren't a perfect match. "Sunni Mason came home a day early and canceled a room from the list, so there's really no reason for me to stay."

Brendan hadn't given her one.

Lily's hands trembled as she folded a pair of jeans and stuffed them in a corner of her suitcase. The numbness flowing sluggishly through her veins made her movements clumsy.

"You love him, don't you?"

"No." *Yes.* "That would be crazy. We hardly know each other."

"Crazy but not impossible. My dad claimed he knew he was going to marry my mother on their first date."

"There you go. Technically, Brendan and I haven't even *had* a first date."

And they never would.

"Technically?" Shelby teased.

Lily was glad her friend couldn't see her blush. "He isn't interested in a relationship. He's interested in work."

And there wasn't room for anything else.

"Brendan Kane isn't your father," Shelby said quietly. "You have to give him a chance."

I did, Lily thought.

"His life is here in Castle Falls, building canoes," Lily said out loud. "I work at Pinnacle."

If her job was still waiting for her when she returned. Lily had tried to set up a meeting with the client from Chicago for after her return only to be informed that Dennis had assigned Paul, a coworker who'd been vying for the same promotion as Lily, to the project. She'd also gone against a direct order from her boss and advised Brendan not to sign the contract.

Not that it had done any good.

"What's next in line when I get back?" Lily asked lightly. "Because I expect you to put me to work on the weekends. I've mastered the whole faux-leather-look thing, and I can't wait to show off my skills."

"Actually, I had a checkup yesterday, and Dr. Gillett gave me the green light to resume my normal activities when I felt better...listen for the drum roll now." Shelby paused. "And I feel better."

"That's great news, Shel." Tears burned the back of Lily's eyes. "But are you sure you aren't rushing things?"

"I'm itching to get paint on my hands again and it's time you got your life back."

Her life.

Lily thought of her too-crowded desk and too-empty apartment. Neither one held any appeal. In two short weeks, Castle Falls, her temporary home, had taken up a permanent place in her heart. Along with a certain frustrating man with blue eyes and a smile that had the power to knock Lily's heart right off its footings.

"Call me the minute you get into town," Shelby commanded. "I'll break out the mint chocolate chip, and you can show me all the photos you took while you were in Castle Falls. I'll make a scrapbook for you, too."

"That would be great." Lily injected as much enthusiasm as she could into the words, knowing a one-dimensional photograph could never capture the crisp scent of the pines or the soothing lullaby the river sang outside her bedroom window when she crawled into bed at night.

She hung up the phone and zipped the suitcase shut. Missy, who'd padded into the room while she was packing, didn't stir inside her nest of pillows at the foot of the bed.

The floorboards squeaked as Lily tiptoed past Sunni's room and made her way downstairs. Brendan's mother had turned in early, and there was no sign of Brendan or his brothers, either.

Good. If everyone had turned in for the night, no one would know that she hadn't. She stopped at the door to Brendan's office and hoped he hadn't locked it this time.

It took a moment for her eyes to adjust, the room lit only by the silver moon peeking under the hem of a cloud.

Lily dragged in a breath, said a prayer and pulled the door shut behind her.

There was one more thing she had to do.

Chapter Twenty-One

Gravel crunched under Brendan's feet as he walked toward the shop. He glanced at the apartment above the garage but the windows were dark. His brothers had probably turned in hours ago. At least someone in the family was able to get some shut-eye.

His hand curled around the doorknob and he gave it a quick twist, feeling like an intruder.

Brendan didn't bother to flip the light switch. A full moon washed the walls in silver, more breathtaking than any faux finish Lily could have applied.

He retreated to his brothers' domain in the back room. A smile twisted Brendan's lips. A narrow wooden table separated Liam and Aiden's workspaces, chaos from order. And yet they managed to work together in harmony for hours on end. While he was ensconced in the office, separated from the day-to-day, hands-on work his brothers enjoyed. Dividing the work had made sense, at least that's what Brendan had told himself at the time.

I was under the impression this was a family business.

Liam's statement still hadn't lost its sting.

God...

The prayer bumped up against an internal wall and Brendan felt the vibrations rattle all the way through him. Along with the realization that he didn't even know where to begin.

How had that happened? How did a man drift so far that he'd forgotten how to find his way back?

A gold frame next to the coffeepot caught Brendan's eye and he picked it up. Underneath the glass, a yellowed newspaper clipping with tattered edges.

Rich smiled back at him.

Brendan's hand shook as he read the headline. "Local Man Sets a New Course."

Under the caption, a story the local newspaper had printed when Rich started Castle Fall Outfitters.

"On the river, there's room to breathe. A man can connect with God...or himself...or maybe even someone he cares about. On a really good day, well, it might be all three."

Brendan could almost hear Rich's booming voice and a moist heat blurred the newsprint.

"I wanted to finish what you started," Brendan whispered. "I wanted to do something that would make you proud."

The shadows in the room shifted, and Brendan spun around.

Brendan hadn't heard Sunni come in, but then

again, pink chenille bedroom slippers provided a person with added stealth.

"Why aren't you sleeping?"

"For the same reason you aren't, I imagine," his mother countered, stifling a yawn with the back of her hand. She tipped her head to see the photograph in his hand. "I always loved that article. Rich didn't want to be interviewed. He didn't understand what all the fuss was about."

No, because his foster dad lived his life from the inside out and was completely unaware how rare that was.

"He *was* proud of you, sweetheart," Sunni said quietly.

Brendan flinched. She'd heard. "Why? All I did was turn your lives upside down."

A smile bloomed on his mother's face. "God must have known we needed a new perspective."

"No one else did." The words were out before Brendan could stop them.

"There were a few people who didn't understand, that's true," Sunni said after a moment. "But we prayed about it and knew it was the right choice."

The words, meant to be comforting, only reminded Brendan of his last conversation with Lily.

It's my choice.

He hadn't even asked the Lord for guidance.

"It was my fault he ended up in the hospital," Brendan said.

Sunni's smile disappeared. "What on earth are you talking about?"

"It wasn't a coincidence he ended up in the hospital the same day I ended up in jail."

Brendan had done his best to stay under the radar after the stolen-watch incident, but Les and his buddies weren't finished with him yet. He may not have decorated the walls of the gym with spray paint, but he had given Les a bloody nose when he caught the guy sneaking the empty can in his locker. Of course the coach hadn't seen that part. The principal called Les's father, who'd called the police. All the way to the police department, Brendan berated himself for losing his temper—and proving everyone was right about him.

"The doctor said that stress wasn't good for his heart," Brendan pushed the words out.

"And you assumed…" Sunni closed her eyes. "Rich knew you hadn't done anything. He mentioned that his chest hurt before he went to bed the night before. If anyone is to blame it would be me for not insisting he go to the clinic and get checked out."

"It's not your fault."

"It's not yours, either." Sunni studied him. "There's more, isn't there? What haven't you told me?"

"The day Rich died…he made me promise. He was so weak, I couldn't make out all the words, but he talked about you. He said something about helping you finish what he started."

Sunni pressed a hand to her mouth. The tears that

filled her eyes brought down an avalanche of regret. Why hadn't he kept that information to himself? It was his burden to carry.

"I'm afraid if we lose this contract, we'll eventually lose everything he worked for—"

"Rich wasn't talking about the business," Sunni interrupted. "He was talking about *you*. We had already started the adoption proceedings. If he said something about a promise, it was a promise he'd made to you. To give you and your brothers a home. With us."

"Why?" Brendan choked.

"Because he loved you."

The room blurred.

Sunni raised up on tiptoes and kissed his cheek. "Rich wouldn't have used his last moments on earth to make sure the business would thrive. He wanted to make sure *you* did."

Brendan couldn't move. Couldn't speak.

"And just because it bears repeating, I love you, too," Sunni said.

Her footsteps faded, leaving Brendan alone.

Except he didn't feel alone.

God, I'm sorry. I messed up. With You. With my family. With Lily. Thank You for not giving up on me.

The words took wing as effortlessly as an eagle taking flight. As effortlessly as breathing.

Brendan opened his eyes and looked at the headline again.

Maybe it was time for him to set a new course, too.

* * *

"Are you sure you don't want some company?"

"No, thanks." Lily took the life jacket from Aiden. "I won't be gone long."

"Mom's making waffles to celebrate your victory over the wallpaper sheep." Liam pushed the canoe into the river and propped one foot against the gunwale to hold it steady. "You don't want to miss out."

"It's a long drive and my friend is expecting me for dinner tonight." Lily averted her gaze. It was the truth, but not the real reason she planned to get an early start. "I'm going to take a few more pictures, and then I'd better hit the road."

"Give us a holler when you get back, then. We'll help you pack up," Aiden offered.

Already done, but Lily scraped up a smile. As much as she appreciated what Brendan's brothers were trying to do, their kindness only made it more difficult to leave.

Her plan to sneak a canoe onto the river without anyone noticing was foiled when Aiden showed up with a thermos of coffee and a bright pink life jacket. Both of them, it turned out, were for her. Liam joined them a few minutes later and didn't even ask what was going on. Just yanked a green canoe from the line.

Lily was going to miss them. And Sunni, even though she'd officially met the woman less than twenty-four hours ago.

She'd heard the low rumble of masculine voices

in the kitchen while packing her suitcase and wondered if Brendan had told his family about the partnership with Extreme Adventures.

Had they embraced the proposal? Or, like her, been unsettled by the thought of removing their logo from the canoes?

None of your business, Lily, remember?

She sat down on the webbed seat and pressed her paddle into the sand, using it as a lever to push the canoe farther into the current.

"Thank you." She hoped Liam and Aiden understood the words encompassed a whole lot more than carrying her canoe down to the water.

"Lily…" Liam rubbed the back of his neck. "Don't stop praying, okay?"

"I won't." Lily's throat felt scratchy. He had understood.

Brendan might not appreciate what he considered her interference, but that wouldn't stop Lily from asking God to intervene.

She just wished she would be there to see the results.

Fresh paint.

Brendan's nose began to sting the moment he walked into the house.

He could hear Sunni humming while she moved around the kitchen but didn't deviate from his course.

The door to his office was open a crack, and Brendan's heart jumped into his throat as he pushed it open. Was Lily waiting for him?

His breath escaped on a ragged sigh when he realized the room was empty. Compared to the rest of the house, his office felt like a cave, the dark green walls absorbed the sunlight but didn't give anything back. Brendan hadn't noticed that before.

He walked over to his desk to fire up the computer and spotted a plain manila envelope propped against it. No name. No address. But somehow he knew Lily had left it there.

Sliding his finger underneath the flap, Brendan pulled out a slim black folder.

The chair squawked in protest when Brendan slumped into it.

His pulse picked up speed, trying to keep up with his fingers as he flipped through the papers inside.

How had Lily known exactly what he'd needed? Especially when, up until a few hours ago, Brendan hadn't had a clue?

Right before he'd fallen asleep, he had asked God to show him what to do.

And here it was. A detailed, professional marketing plan that must have kept Lily up most of the night.

Brendan reread one of the proposals and a wry smile tipped his lips. Okay, so an answer to prayer didn't necessarily go hand in hand with easy. Or comfortable. Because Lily's business plan included a whole slew of ideas and every one of them meant inviting people right to his front door—and the river that ran past it. Canoeing lessons. Day trips. Overnight camping. School field trips...

Field trips?

Brendan thought about the soccer team and how he'd actually had fun filling in as their coach. Yeah, he supposed they could do that, too.

There was also a list of Christian camps located in the Midwest that specialized in wilderness experiences. All good stuff...

The last paper crinkled in Brendan's hands.

Lily had scanned in an old photograph of Rich that she must have noticed on the coffee table in the living room. A lanky teenager in jeans and a flannel shirt at the time it was taken, Rich stood next to the first canoe he'd ever made. A masterpiece handcrafted from wood and canvas.

Not just a canoe...it's a feeling.

Lily had written the words next to Rich's photo.

Brendan laughed out loud, seeing Lily's humor peeking through. He'd claimed you couldn't run a business on emotion and she'd shown him the two weren't mutually exclusive.

She'd shown him a lot of things.

He read the outline underneath the caption, promoting Castle Falls Outfitters new line of classic wood canoes.

Liam would flip. In fact, Brendan wondered why they'd never thought of it before. The plan would require a lot of work and a fair amount of risk. There were no guarantees it would be successful...unless you had a different definition of the word.

Brendan vaulted to his feet. As he reached the door, it swung open and almost cracked him in the nose. Aiden and Liam filed in. Brendan snagged his younger brother's arm.

"Have you seen Lily?"

"She left."

Left?

Aiden and Liam glanced at each other.

"She said she wanted to get an early start."

"You *talked* to her?"

"Uh-huh." Aiden shrugged. "What's the problem?"

"The problem is..." Brendan raked his hand through his hair. "I had to tell her...something important."

Liam crossed his arms. "That you messed up?"

"And you're an idiot?" Aiden added.

His brothers had always been honest with him. Brendan decided it was time to return the favor. "Yes," he admitted. "And that I love her."

Aiden grinned. "If you leave now, you can probably catch up with her."

Brendan stared at his brother in disbelief. "I'm supposed to chase her down on the highway?"

"Nope." Liam pointed at the canoes. "With one of those."

Perched on the stone ledge of a wishing well, Lily tipped her head back and watched a hawk stretch out its wings and coast above the treetops.

Why had she delayed the inevitable? She should have ignored the sudden impulse to take a canoe out one last time. In half an hour, Brendan would make his way to the office and find the envelope she'd left.

Would he laugh? Toss it into the nearest wastebasket?

Lily decided it didn't matter. All she knew was that she couldn't ignore the internal nudge—telling her to give Brendan another option. What he did with it was up to him.

A kingfisher searching for breakfast suddenly took to the air and rattled out a warning, which was immediately picked up by its mate and carried down the river like a teletype machine.

Lily shaded her eyes against the sun and saw a canoe cutting a path through the water. Her heart began to pound in double time when she recognized the man paddling toward her.

Brendan's canoe glided into the small bay. Unless Lily dove into the brush and took off cross-country, she was neatly trapped.

Neither of them spoke as Brendan hopped out of his canoe and climbed up the rocks.

Lily laced her fingers together in her lap, not sure what to say. She was all too aware of him as he settled beside her.

Was Brendan here to say goodbye? Or had he seen the envelope? Lily sneaked a look at him from under her lashes but it was impossible to read his expression.

"I guess paddling a canoe is like riding a bike," he said after a moment. "You don't forget how."

Curiosity got the better of Lily. "When was the last time you took one out on the river?"

"Fourteen years ago."

Lily couldn't hide her astonishment. "Why?"

"I tried. Once. But all I could think about was how much Rich loved to be on the river and I felt guilty that I was able to do something he couldn't."

"I didn't know him, but I don't think Rich would have wanted you to feel guilty. I think he would have wanted you to enjoy God's creation, the way he did."

"That proves you know him better than I did." Brendan picked up a rock and rolled it between his fingers. "I got into some trouble at school and ended up at the police station the day Rich had a heart attack."

"What happened?" Lily asked softly.

"One of my classmates had it in for me because I had long hair and had the audacity not to have been born here." Brendan's lips twisted in a smile. "It wasn't the first time he'd hassled me and I got tired of it. Lost my temper. He pulled another prank that day…and I threw a punch. I might have gotten away with a detention if he hadn't been a star football player…and the vice principal's son.

"Sunni was crying when she came to pick me up and I figured it was my fault. She said Rich was in the hospital and we needed to get back there. All I could think was how they'd be better off if they had kept Aiden and Liam and sent me back to Detroit. I'd been nothing but trouble.

"A few days after Rich passed away, some of Sunni's friends stopped by the house. I overheard them saying that no one would blame her if she sent those 'foster boys' back to Detroit."

Lily blew out a quiet breath. It explained why Brendan distanced himself from people. It also explained why it was so important that Castle Falls Outfitters succeed. It would prove to everyone they'd been wrong about him.

"But she didn't."

"Sunni told the women we were *her* boys. And to prove it, she legally adopted all three of us."

"Adopted? But your last name is still Kane." After the childhood Aiden had described, Lily was surprised they hadn't changed it.

A shadow crossed Brendan's face. "When I was ten, Mom got pregnant. I have no idea who the baby's father was—ours was long gone by then. She gave the baby—a little girl—up for adoption and never talked about her again. Liam and Aiden were so young, I doubt they even realized what happened, but if she ever tried to find us, she wouldn't be looking for three Mason brothers."

Lily's eyes stung with unshed tears. It was so like Brendan to watch over his family—even the sister he'd never met.

"Your plan… I can't do it, Lily."

He had seen the contents of the envelope. That was why he'd tracked her down.

Tears banked behind her eyes. "I understand—"

"Not without you."

Not without— "What do you mean?"

"I mean I was wrong—about a lot of things. I was fighting the past. My emotions. Pretty much everything." Brendan shook his head. "It might not be fair to ask you to give up everything and move to Castle Falls, but I need you. Here."

"I...don't understand. You're offering me a job?" Blinking back tears, Lily turned to stare at him.

"Yes. No." Brendan rolled his eyes. "I'm not making myself very clear, am I? Maybe this will help."

Before Lily could blink—before she could move—Brendan leaned forward, framed her face in his hands and claimed her lips. Lily closed her eyes and leaned into the kiss, the last of her doubts melting away in the heat of it.

The breath trapped in Lily's lungs only escaped when Brendan released her.

"I don't want to lose you. Stay in Castle Falls and help me make your plan for Castle Falls Outfitters a reality, because I think it's God's plan, too. I love you, Lily," he murmured. "I can't even begin to tell you how much."

"You're off to a pretty good start," Lily said shakily.

Brendan's slow smile took her breath away all over again. So did the warm glow in his eyes, evidence of a peace that could have only come from making peace with the past. And with God.

"Of course, if you stay, we will have to share an office," he told her.

Lily pretended to consider that. "The green walls will have to go."

"I'll help you paint them."

"And the desk… We're going to have to turn it around so it faces the window."

"Done."

Lily smiled. "When can I start?"

"I spent the last thirty years waiting for you," Brendan said, his voice a little unsteady. "How about today?"

"Today." Lily savored the word. "Sounds absolutely perfect."

And tomorrow was looking pretty good, too.

Epilogue

"Everything looks beautiful, Lily."

Anna twirled around and the movement stirred the flames of the candles that graced the linen-covered tables.

"I'm glad you like it." Lily moved a basket of autumn mums a few inches away from the punch bowl.

"Like it?" Anna pulled her in for a hug. "The open house was a wonderful idea. I'm so glad Brendan let me steal you away to help me set it up. Sunni said he's been keeping you busy."

"Stone Creek Camp has been keeping us busy." Lily fiddled with a stack of napkins so her friend wouldn't see her blush. "Thanks to the Vandencourts' donation, they ordered another dozen canoes. Liam and Aiden will be busy all winter."

There it was. The shuttered look that came over Anna's face whenever Liam's name was mentioned.

It hadn't escaped Lily's notice, either, that while Aiden had frequently pitched in during the renovation process, the middle Kane brother always seemed to have an excuse why he couldn't help.

In spite of Liam's curious reluctance to be around Anna, the support for Anna's new business adventure had been overwhelming. This evening was more than an open house, it was a gathering of the people Lily had come to love in the few short months she'd been part of the community.

Anna grabbed her hand. "Tell me what you think. I'm almost finished setting up the display."

Her friend's feet barely touched the floor as they made their way across the room. Strings of white lights winked in the fresh pine boughs scattered down the center of a long table. Nestled in boxes covered in gold paper that captured the light from the antique chandelier were the rings and necklaces Anna had crafted.

"I think you're going to have to hire a manager for the ice cream shop so you can fill the orders you're going to get tonight," Lily said.

"It's your fault, you know." Anna laughed. "You're the one who cheered me on."

"I've been told I'm…enthusiastic."

"And perky." A voice whispered in her ear.

A shiver skated down Lily's spine and she turned—right into Brendan's arms.

"Hello." Lily practically strangled on the word.

It wasn't fair that Brendan had smiling down to an art form now.

"Can you two check the lights on the balcony while I put out the refreshments?" Anna glided away. "They're on a timer and they were supposed to go on a few minutes ago."

"Sure." Lily had barely closed the French doors leading outside when Brendan pulled her into his arms.

"Alone at last." He bent his head, claiming her lips with a soul-stirring kiss that pushed the chilly October temperature up a few degrees.

When he finally released her, Lily grinned up at him.

"What was that for?"

"Because I love you."

She never tired of hearing the words. She turned into his broad chest and breathed in the scent of pine and peppermint.

"I love you back," she murmured.

Instrumental music drifted from speakers hidden in the corners behind bronze vases filled with dark pink sedum and lacey ferns that Rebecca and the book group had gathered on an afternoon jaunt through the woods.

"Sounds like the first guests have arrived." Brendan opened the door and stepped aside. "You're part of the official welcoming committee, right?"

"Right—" Lily pressed her hand against her

mouth when she spotted a familiar figure framed in the doorway.

"Shelby!"

Her friend opened her arms. "Surprise."

"Where... How did you?" Lily looked at Brendan. "You knew about this?"

"He's the one who invited me."

"You look great." Lily searched her friend's face. Shelby still looked pale, but the sparkle in her eyes hadn't dimmed.

"I'm feeling a little stronger every day." Shelby shucked off her jacket and Lily was thrilled to see she'd put on some weight since the last time they'd seen each other. "Did you drive up? How long can you stay? Where are you staying?"

Shelby burst out laughing. "I can stay a few days.... Sunni offered me the guest room right next to yours...and I had a driver."

"A driver?" Lily repeated, not sure if her friend was teasing. "Who?"

Shelby stepped aside. "Someone who's anxious for a tour of your operation."

"Hello, Lily."

"Dad." Lily's knees turned to slush as Nolan Michaels stepped into the room.

Brendan's arm slipped around her waist, providing the strength Lily needed to keep herself upright. She hadn't spoken to her father in over three months, roughly the same amount of time Lily had been living in Castle Falls. Once Nolan had exhausted his list of reasons why she should try to get her job back at Pinnacle, the phone had stopped ringing.

Lily silently grieved the loss of their relationship, even if it had been difficult, but Brendan had noticed. He always noticed.

She squeezed his hand. *It'll be okay,* his eyes said.

"Thought I'd see what you've been up to lately," her father said gruffly. "Maybe take one of those canoes for a test drive."

"You?" Lily blurted.

"Your mother and I...we used to do a little camping before you were born." A memory shimmered in Nolan's eyes. "It was the only thing we could afford."

Lily felt her heart swell. It was a rare thing for her father to open up about the past. Even more rare for him to talk about her mother. She could only pray it signaled a turning point in their relationship.

"Do you want some apple cider?" Cassie Leighton landed in front of them. Like her twin sister, she'd worn a dress for the open house but the rubber toes of her high-top Chuck Taylors peeked below the hem.

Chloe held up a tray. "And peanut butter cookies?"

"I think I'll take a look at Anna's collection." Shelby filched a cookie and ambled away.

Anna motioned to Lily. "This is for you."

Lily opened the slender box and began shaking her head. "Anna, no. I can't take this!"

"All the volunteers are wearing my jewelry to-night." Her eyes twinkled. "My marketing expert would call it free advertising."

"It's beautiful, Anna." Lily knew where her friend had found the violet, now perfectly preserved in the tiny glass charm. The tiny flowers grew near the falls. "Thank you."

"Thank you." Anna hugged her. "You changed my life, you know."

Dumbfounded, Lily watched her friend glide toward another group of people standing in the doorway.

"You seem to have that effect on people," Brendan murmured in her ear.

"I can't believe you invited Shelby and—" Lily's voice hitched "—my dad."

"On second thought, neither can I. We hardly have a minute alone as it is." The frown on Brendan's face didn't touch the smile in his eyes.

"I'll pencil you in," Lily promised.

The look in Brendan's eyes stripped the air from her lungs. "How about now?"

He grabbed her hand and tugged her toward the stairs.

"Where are we going? It's cold out here!"

Lily's musical laughter combined with the crisp October air.

Brendan loved to hear the sound.

He hadn't planned this impromptu getaway until he'd overheard Anna's comment. The bewildered look on Lily's face told him that she had no clue the impact she made on people's lives. She was just... Lily.

The woman who held his heart in her hand.

"Kidnapping is a crime, you know." Lily snuggled against him.

Brendan steered her toward the river. "Then it's a good thing Officer Kirkwell's shift ends at six o'clock."

He felt, rather than saw, Lily's smile.

"Will you help me put this necklace on?" She presented her back to him and stood patiently while Brendan struggled with the tiny clasp.

"What do you think?" Lily touched the tiny charm dangling at the base of her throat.

"It's definitely missing something."

"Missing—" The violet eyes widened in disbelief. "Like what?"

"A little more sparkle." Brendan pulled the small velvet box from his jacket pocket. "Like this."

He opened the lid, a little stunned to realize his hand was shaking.

"Bren..." Lily, at a loss for words.

But then, so was Brendan. Or maybe they couldn't get past the knot in his throat. "Will—"

"Yes!" Lily's eyes sparkled with mischief, brighter than the diamond that winked up at her.

Brendan groaned in mock protest. "You didn't wait for me to say my line."

"Sorry." Lily didn't look sorry at all. "You looked

like you weren't sure what you were supposed to do next."

"That's because I didn't plan this," Brendan admitted.

"There was supposed to be flowers and music and candlelight, but I…changed my mind."

"How very spontaneous of you," Lily whispered as she held out her hand.

"I'm working on it." Brendan slipped the ring on her finger. "You have to promise you'll be patient with me."

"As long as *you* promise that someday we'll bring our kids down here and tell them how their daddy proposed—"

Brendan pulled Lily into his arms and kissed her again.

Because that was a promise he would have no trouble keeping at all.

* * * * *

Dear Reader,

I like to think of nature as God's classroom. A canoe trip down the river—in the name of research, of course!—reminded me how important it is to seek His direction. Too many times, I try to set my own course and life gets out of balance. Trusting in God's goodness calms my heart even when I'm in the middle of the rapids. It's my prayer you'll seek His presence on your journey!

It's always exciting to launch a new series and I hope you are looking forward to your next visit to Castle Falls. Brendan Kane and his brothers are my favorite kind of heroes—men who want to build a strong foundation on faith and family. But that doesn't mean it will be easy, as Liam Kane discovers in the next book!

As always, I'd love to hear your feedback. Please stop by my website at www.kathrynspringer.com and sign up to receive my free eNewsletter, or write to me in care of Love Inspired at 233 Broadway, New York, NY 10279.

Keep smiling and seeking Him!

Kathryn Springer

Questions for Discussion

1. Lily Michaels put her life on hold to help out a friend. Have you ever done that for someone? What were the circumstances?

2. Why did Brendan keep the people in Castle Falls at a distance? What did that decision cost him?

3. Rich Mason left behind a rich legacy. How do you want people to remember you?

4. In what ways could Lily relate to Brendan? What qualities did they share? How were they different?

5. Read *Psalms* 1. How would you define the word *prosperity?* How did Brendan's interpretation differ from his foster dad's?

6. Do you agree with Brendan's reason for keeping the contract with Extreme Adventures a secret? Under what circumstances do you feel it is all right to withhold information from a friend or family member?

7. Discuss Lily's and Brendan's childhoods and the impact it had on the decisions they made as adults.

8. What are some of the things you wish you had more time for?

9. What was significant about the fact that Brendan's desk faced the wall instead of the window?

10. What was the turning point in Brendan and Lily's relationship?

11. Both Lily and Brendan sought solitude in the cave by the falls. Do you have a special place where you retreat to think, pray or recharge? Where is it?

12. Who is your favorite character? Why?

13. Do you think Brendan made the right decision when he chose Lily's plan instead of his own?

14. What was your favorite scene in the book?

15. What are three words you think people would use to describe you? What are three words you would *like* people to use to describe you?

LARGER-PRINT BOOKS!

GET 2 FREE
LARGER-PRINT NOVELS
PLUS 2 FREE
MYSTERY GIFTS

RIVETING INSPIRATIONAL ROMANCE

Larger-print novels are now available...

YES! Please send me 2 FREE LARGER-PRINT Love Inspired® Suspense novels and my 2 FREE mystery gifts (gifts are worth about $10). After receiving them, if I don't wish to receive any more books, I can return the shipping statement marked "cancel." If I don't cancel, I will receive 4 brand-new novels every month and be billed just $5.24 per book in the U.S. or $5.74 per book in Canada. That's a savings of at least 23% off the cover price. It's quite a bargain! Shipping and handling is just 50¢ per book in the U.S. and 75¢ per book in Canada.* I understand that accepting the 2 free books and gifts places me under no obligation to buy anything. I can always return a shipment and cancel at any time. Even if I never buy another book, the two free books and gifts are mine to keep forever.

110/310 IDN F5CC

Name _____ (PLEASE PRINT) _____

Address _____ Apt. # _____

City _____ State/Prov. _____ Zip/Postal Code _____

Signature (if under 18, a parent or guardian must sign) _____

Mail to the **Harlequin® Reader Service:**
IN U.S.A.: P.O. Box 1867, Buffalo, NY 14240-1867
IN CANADA: P.O. Box 609, Fort Erie, Ontario L2A 5X3

Are you a current subscriber to Love Inspired Suspense books and want to receive the larger-print edition?
Call 1-800-873-8635 or visit www.ReaderService.com.

* Terms and prices subject to change without notice. Prices do not include applicable taxes. Sales tax applicable in N.Y. Canadian residents will be charged applicable taxes. Offer not valid in Quebec. This offer is limited to one order per household. Not valid for current subscribers to Love Inspired Suspense larger-print books. All orders subject to credit approval. Credit or debit balances in a customer's account(s) may be offset by any other outstanding balance owed by or to the customer. Please allow 4 to 6 weeks for delivery. Offer available while quantities last.

Your Privacy—The Harlequin® Reader Service is committed to protecting your privacy. Our Privacy Policy is available online at www.ReaderService.com or upon request from the Harlequin Reader Service.

We make a portion of our mailing list available to reputable third parties that offer products we believe may interest you. If you prefer that we not exchange your name with third parties, or if you wish to clarify or modify your communication preferences, please visit us at www.ReaderService.com/consumerchoice or write to us at Harlequin Reader Service Preference Service, P.O. Box 9062, Buffalo, NY 14269. Include your complete name and address.

LISLPDIR13R

ReaderService.com

Manage your account online!

- Review your order history
- Manage your payments
- Update your address

*We've designed
the Harlequin® Reader Service
website just for you.*

Enjoy all the features!

- Reader excerpts from any series
- Respond to mailings and
  special monthly offers
- Discover new series available to you
- Browse the Bonus Bucks catalog
- Share your feedback

Visit us at:
ReaderService.com